THE BATTLES OF TOLKIEN

To my mother, Jean Day

Thunder Bay Press
An imprint of Printers Row Publishing Group
9717 Pacific Heights Blvd, San Diego, CA 92121
www.thunderbaybooks.com • mail@thunderbaybooks.com

Text copyright © David Day 2016, 2017, 2019
Artwork, design and layout copyright Octopus Publishing Group Ltd © 2016, 2017, 2019

Printers Row Publishing Group is a division of Readerlink Distribution Services, LLC.
Thunder Bay Press is a registered trademark of Readerlink Distribution Services, LLC.

Correspondence regarding the content of this book should be sent to Thunder Bay Press, Editorial Department, at the above address. Author and rights inquiries should be addressed to Octopus Publishing Group Ltd Carmelite House, 50 Victoria Embankment, London EC4Y 0DZ www.octopusbooks.co.uk

THUNDER BAY PRESS
Publisher: Peter Norton
Associate Publisher: Ana Parker
Publishing/Editorial Team: April Farr, Kelly Larsen, Kathryn C. Dalby
Editorial Team: JoAnn Padgett, Melinda Allman, Traci Douglas, Dan Mansfield

PYRAMID
Publisher: Lucy Pessell
Design Manager: Megan van Staden
Design: Amazing15
Editor: Natalie Bradley
Project Editor: Anna Bowles
Administrative Assistant: Sarah Vaughan
Senior Production Manager: Peter Hunt

Illustrations by Victor Ambrus (cover), Jacopo Ascari (maps), Graham Bence, Jaroslav Bradac, Tim Clarey, Allan Curless, Gino D'Achille, David Franklin, Melvin Grant, Sam Hadley, David Kearney, Barbara Lofthouse, Mauro Mazzara, Ian Miller, Sue Porter, Lidia Postma, David Roberts

ISBN: 978-1-64517-927-6

Printed in China

26 25 24 23 22 2 3 4 5 6

~THE~
BATTLES
~OF~
TOLKIEN

DAVID DAY

THUNDER BAY
P · R · E · S · S
San Diego, California

CONTENTS

———◆◆◆———

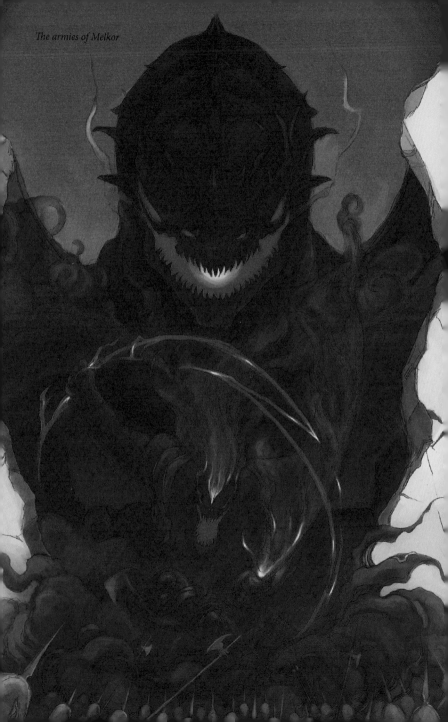

The armies of Melkor

From the creation of J.R.R. Tolkien's world of Arda until the end of the War of the Rings – some 37,000* years later – cataclysmic wars punctuated by crucial battles have determined the course of that world's evolution and history. In the recording of these events upon Middle-earth and the Undying Lands, Tolkien takes a similar approach to that of a real-world historian.

Like those of their real-life historic counterparts, the annals of Tolkien's races and nations record each civilization's achievements in the creative arts, the architecture of its great cities and the genius of its technologies, but they also give weight to the pivotal role of great battles that result in the rise and fall of empires.

---

* This estimation of 37,000 years is based on one early version of Tolkien's own chronology. However, there is another (and possibly earlier) account by Tolkien that suggests a 57,000-year history. That said, the disputed 20,000 years occur so early in Arda's history that virtually no specific events take place. Consequently, I have chosen to stick with Tolkien's first published time span.

For undeniably it is in battles and wars that the fates of nations and races are finally determined. And for all nations (both real and imaginary), it is in these crucial battles that the courage and wisdom of their most celebrated heroes are ultimately tested. Furthermore, these wars are also the crucial themes of all the great civilizations' national epics: Greece's *Iliad*, Germany's *Nibelungenlied*, Norway and Iceland's *Elder Edda*, India's *Mahabharata*, Mesopotamia's *Epic of Gilgamesh*.

In Tolkien's Middle-earth, *The Lord of the Rings* is certainly comparable to Greece's *Iliad*. However, the difference is that Homer – unlike Tolkien – did not have to invent an entire world's evolution, geography, history and mythology before even beginning his tale of the Trojan War.

In *The Battles of Tolkien* we take a close-up view of the wars and battles that took place in Arda over its 37,000 years of history. We look into the forces, weaponry and tactics that came into play on these epic battlegrounds where the fate of Tolkien's races, nations and civilizations were determined. These often invite comparisons to real-world battles

The Elven city of Tirion

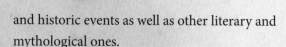

and historic events as well as other literary and mythological ones.

There have been other attempts to re-create the battles, combatants and battlegrounds. However, this book is unique in combining all these elements with a high level of artwork and a commentary that provides the reader with an understanding of J.R.R. Tolkien's moral and philosophical perspective on these cataclysmic events. For as entertaining as it may be to examine Tolkien's battles as a colourful series of war games, his dramatic accounts of these conflicts are so much more than variations of battles in a game of *Dungeons & Dragons*.

As we shall see, Tolkien's wars are concerned with moral conflicts related to his view of the nature of good and evil. For, as he once observed: 'Myth and fairy-story must, as all art, reflect and contain in solution elements of moral and religious truth.' And although battle lines in these wars are clearly drawn, they are not simplistic. As Elrond Half-elven explained: 'Nothing is evil in the beginning. Even Sauron was not so.' We are informed that 'evil' Orcs and Trolls were bred from 'good' Elves and Ents. And even Balrogs were once brilliant, angelic Maiar spirits of fire.

It is Tolkien's moral philosophy, and his complex portrayal of the psychological nature of good and evil (a complexity most obviously portrayed in the split personality of Sméagol/Gollum), that makes these wars and battles so much more than a diverting drama about the deeds of heroes.

Tolkien's wars are fought over the conflict inherent in the struggle between the morally just right to rule and the corruption implicit in a desire for power for its own sake. This, in turn, is based on a philosophical conflict resulting from a belief in the idea of free will coupled with the counter-intuitive belief in fate and a submission to a divine plan.

In the real world, Tolkien was a royalist in the Victorian sense that he believed in rule by a hereditary constitutional monarch. However, in his created world of Middle-earth, he accepts the medieval fairy-tale tradition of a right to rule based on the semi-divine descent of kings. This is combined with a perspective in keeping with the historian Thomas Carlyle's view that the 'history of the world is but the biography of great men'.

For, certainly, at critical moments in Tolkien's annals of Middle-earth, 'great men' (or women) inevitably arise (for good or ill) to shape the course of its history.

In *The Lord of the Rings*, Aragorn is the prototype of this hero who arises from relative obscurity, but by virtue of his courage – and an inherent ability to command – is able to seize the day and set the world to rights.

However, in Middle-earth, Tolkien tempers these tales of archetypal heroes with a much more human and humane view of the machinery of fate. In the War of the Ring, in particular, the tides of battles are turned not by the deeds of obvious heroes or villains, but by the action of the most unlikely and unheroic of individuals. Indeed, as Tolkien himself once stated: 'the great policies of world history, "the wheels of the world", are often turned not by the Lords and Governors, even gods, but by the seemingly unknown and weak.' In Tolkien's world, it is these accidental heroes who – by 'chance' or 'luck' – appear at pivotal moments and prove to be the true vehicles of what we may ultimately recognize as 'destiny' or 'fate'.

One word of caution about the maps in
The Battles of Tolkien: they are works of art born
of the imagination of creative artists, informed by
J.R.R. Tolkien's books. These maps are illustrations
that are no less interpretative of sources than
other original illustrations of the characters,
creatures and landscapes in this book – and
therefore can be seen as well informed, but not
authoritative.

All in all, the maps, illustrations, charts
and commentaries in *The Battles of Tolkien* are
meant as guides and aids to the reading and
comprehension of Tolkien's works. However, they
are no substitute for reading the full and vivid
accounts of these epic battles in the original texts.
Consequently, for each battle, references are given
back to the original texts and principal sources in
J.R.R. Tolkien's books.

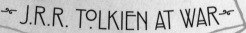

~ J.R.R. TOLKIEN AT WAR ~

War is a constant aspect of J.R.R. Tolkien's imaginary world. This was undoubtedly related to his experience of two world wars and his studies of European literature (particularly Anglo-Saxon epic poetry) and ancient European military history.

- *1914* Britain declares war on Germany. Tolkien defers enlistment until he can complete his degree.

- *1915* Enlists in the volunteer army and is commissioned as a second lieutenant in the 13th Lancashire Fusiliers. Trains as a signalling officer.

- *1916* Travels to France for further signals training. Transferred to the 11th Lancashire Fusiliers. Participates in two offences in the Battle of the Somme in which over a million Allied and Axis soldiers are slaughtered. Invalided home with 'trench fever' – probably saving his life.

- *1917* Tolkien continues to suffer from severe typhoid-like symptoms of trench fever. Begins writing *Siege of Gondolin* and other tales of what will eventually become *The Silmarillion*.

- *1918* Tolkien remains partially invalided in Britain, where he is posted to home service camps. Promoted to lieutenant.
- *1920* Awarded the post of Reader in English Language at the University of Leeds.
- *1925* Appointed Rawlinson and Bosworth Professor of Anglo-Saxon at Oxford; holds post for the next 20 years.
- *1937* Publication of *The Hobbit*.
- *1938* Begins sequel to *The Hobbit* that slowly evolves into *The Lord of the Rings*.
- *1939–1945* The Second World War. Tolkien describes Hitler as a 'ruddy little ignoramus' for ruining and perverting the noble northern spirit of Germanic tradition. Tolkien continues to write *The Lord of the Rings*. Two of his sons, Michael and Christopher, see military service. Michael is injured during training as an aircraft gunner, but survives. War ends in Europe: then Japan. Tolkien is horrified and stunned by news of the detonation of the first atomic bombs. He considers it utter folly.
- *1954–1955* Publication of *The Lord of the Rings*.
- *1977* Publication of *The Silmarillion*.

PART
ONE

BATTLES

OF THE

VALARIAN

AGES

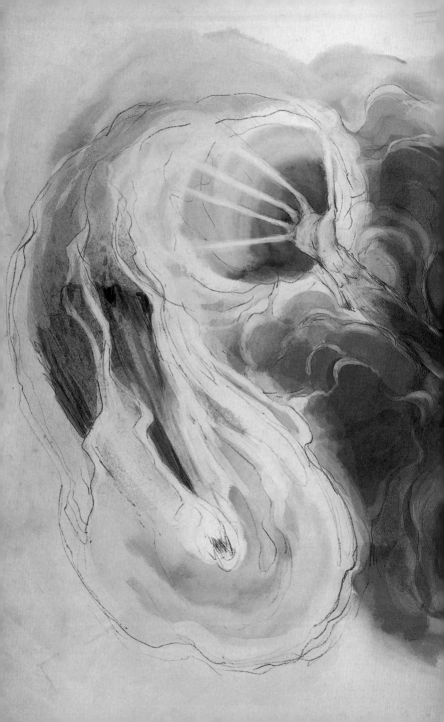

The creation of Arda

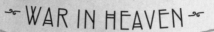

⁓ WAR IN HEAVEN ⁓

I n *The Silmarillion*, Tolkien presents the reader with the genesis of his universe, in which there is a great battle before the beginning of time and the actual creation of his world. Such a conflict, Tolkien informs us, is essential to any tale: 'There cannot be any "story" without a fall – all stories are ultimately about the fall.' And so, right from the conception of his cosmogony, his model of the origin of the universe, 'there is a fall: a fall of Angels'.

In this portrayal of a war in heaven fought by angelic powers, Tolkien is drawing on a theme common to the origin myths of most of the world's great belief systems. In Christianity, it has its origin in the Revelation to John, in which the angels, led into battle by the Archangel Michael, defeat the fallen angels of Satan who are thrown down from the heavens.

The Creator in Tolkien's cosmos is Eru the One, whose angels are the offspring of his thought, and are known as the Ainur, the Holy Ones. His satanic angel is Melkor, whose name means 'He Who Arises in Might'; while Manwë, 'the Blessed One', is the Ainu equivalent of the Archangel Michael. And the battleground for this conflict was an eternal dimension, created by Eru Ilúvatar, the Father of All, known as the Timeless Halls.

Like Tolkien's Ainur, war among St John's angels is interpreted as a battle in heaven fought at the beginning of time – which was (again as in Tolkien) believed to mirror another great battle at the end of time. And well beyond the specific textual references to Revelation, this theme of a war among angels is strongly supported by passages in the Hebrew Bible, and in extensive portrayals of angels battling in heaven throughout centuries of Christian art.

In literature, the war in heaven has been most famously portrayed in John Milton's *Paradise Lost*, in which Lucifer leads an army of rebel angels against God, only to be defeated and hurled down from the heavens. In Tolkien, it is Melkor who rebels against Eru in the Timeless Halls. Both these struggles relate to the moral forces inherent in creation that foreshadow the wars and battles of a world yet to come. Tolkien's account is totally original and differs from every other creation myth: his war in heaven is fought as a battle of voices in an angelic choir, the Ainur, as they perform the great music conceived by Eru the One.

In the Music of the Ainur, there arises an element of strife led by Melkor, which becomes a war of sound: a mighty conflict of opposing themes of harmony and discord that weaves the future of Arda. Ultimately, in Tolkien's cosmos, music is the organizing principle behind all creation.

Yet, as original as Tolkien's Music of the Ainur is as a creation myth, its conception is entirely consistent with another ancient theme known as the Music of the Spheres. This is one of the oldest and most sustained themes in European intellectual life: a belief in a metaphysical musico-mathematical system attributed to the ancient Greek mystic Pythagoras and the philosopher Plato that was central to art and science for more than two thousand years. The Music of the Spheres was a sublimely harmonious system of a cosmos guided by a supreme intelligence that was preordained and eternal.

Although belief in this system has faded since the Industrial Revolution and the advancements of science, even during Tolkien's lifetime – and since – this grand theme has inspired composers and artists as an expression of celestial harmony and a sense of order in the universe.

In Tolkien, the Music of the Ainur is a prehistory of his world that foretells all the wars in the coming civilizations of Elves and Men, a system that, as with the Music of the Spheres, both allows the existence of free will and presupposes that, at the beginning of time, all future battles between the forces of good and evil are encoded within a celestial music.

THE
FIRST
WAR

DATE: AGES OF THE VALAR

LOCATION: ARDA

L ittle can be told of the discord in the Music
of the Ainur because, although Tolkien's
account of that war in the heavens is vastly
operatic in nature, it is an ethereal conflict
in a timeless dimension that no mortal could
comprehend.

However, once the Ainur entered Arda, Tolkien
tells us that these angelic spirits could choose
to take on shape and form by putting on 'the
raiment of Earth'. And in these forms they might
be recognized as 'beings of the same order of
beauty, power and majesty as the "gods" of higher
mythology'. They became known as the Valar and
the Maiar, and they began to shape the world. In
this, Tolkien's Arda has much in common with
myths worldwide, which explain geography as a
result of a war among supernatural beings.

In the ancient Greek Titanomachy, much of the
Greek world was given shape as Titans and giants
fought against the gods. As the Titans would stack
mountains upon mountains to gain advantage
over the Olympians, so in Tolkien's First War the
conflict between Melkor and the Valar toppled
mountains and boiled seas, leading to the Marring
of Arda. War ceased only when the Valar called

upon Tulkas the Strong, the equivalent of the Greek Heracles, who was so formidable that Melkor declined to challenge him, and instead passed into the darkness of the Void.

The opposition of light to the darkness of chaos plays a key part in Greek creation myths, and so it is with Tolkien. In the aftermath of war, the Valar raised the two Great Pillars of the Lamps of Light: Illuin in the north and Helcar in the south, and founded their first kingdom on the Isle of Almaren. Likewise, the Greek gods founded Olympus in a world where four pillars of light held the sky apart from the Earth.

However, this long peace was eventually broken after Melkor secretly reentered Arda and toppled the Great Lamps. Once again, the return of light in Tolkien's world symbolized the reestablishment of order, as the Valar created the realm of Valinor and raised two mighty Trees of Light – one of silver and one of gold. In later ages, these were to bear the fruit that became the Sun and the Moon, an idea perhaps rooted in the myth of the Garden of the Hesperides where, as W.B. Yeats wrote, enchanted trees bore 'The silver apples of the moon / The golden apples of the sun.'

Aulë, Maker of Mountains

THE BATTLE OF POWERS

DATE: AGES OF THE STARS

LOCATION: NORTHWEST MIDDLE-EARTH

T he Battle of Powers was the climactic conflict
that brought an end to the long War for the
Sake of the Elves in the Ages of the Stars.
It was a battle that has its literary precedence in
Greco-Roman mythology, as well as parallels with
religious folklore.

Although far more powerful, the Valarian
Queen Varda Elentári (meaning 'Noble Queen
of the Stars') had an ancient Greek progenitrix
in Astraea (meaning 'Star-Maiden'), who was
associated with the constellation Virgo. It was
Varda who rekindled the stars above Middle-
earth, so awakening the Elves.

The Elves awoke far to the east of Middle-earth,
so were unseen by the distant Valar, but Melkor
discovered them. Through captivity and torture
he twisted them into the cannibal goblin race of
the Orcs. In this, Tolkien enriched and darkened
the ogres who are familiar to us from fairy tales.
As he explained: 'Orc I derived from Anglo-Saxon
– a word meaning demon.' The term originated as
orcos, spirits from the underworld ruled over by
the ancient Romano-Etruscan god Orcus, and was
used for the cannibal demons known as 'orcs' in
Anglo-Saxon before reaching us as 'ogres'.

In Tolkien's story, it was for the salvation of the Elves that the Valar returned to Middle-earth to make war on Melkor. Just as Zeus, the king of the gods, led the Olympians into the War of the Gods and Giants, so Manwë, the king of the Valar, led the Host of the Valar against Melkor. And just as the Olympians overwhelmed and laid waste to the giants' mountain fortress of Ossa, so the Valar overwhelmed and laid waste to Melkor's rebel Maiar and his 'iron fortress' of Angband.

The Host of the Valar then laid siege to Melkor's greatest fortress of Utumno. Before the gates, Melkor (or Morgoth, as he was now known) was forced to come forth in open combat with

Tulkas the Strong in a test of strength reminiscent of Heracles's famous Olympian victory over the invincible wrestler, Antaios the Giant, and Melkor was defeated. Like the rebel Titans and giants held captive by the Greek god Hades (Roman Pluto) in the vaults of Tartarus, so Morgoth was held for many ages in the deep underground Halls of Mandos, the Master of Doom.

Meanwhile, the Valar offered the Eldar the choice of whether to stay in their land, Cuiviénen, or journey to dwell in the Undying Lands. In this, Tolkien shows the difference between his powers and the gods of classical mythology: although some could be fickle, such as Ossë, master of the waves, who delighted in shipwrecks, the greatest

NEXT PAGE
*Tulkas the Strong challenges Morgoth,
the 'Dark Enemy'*

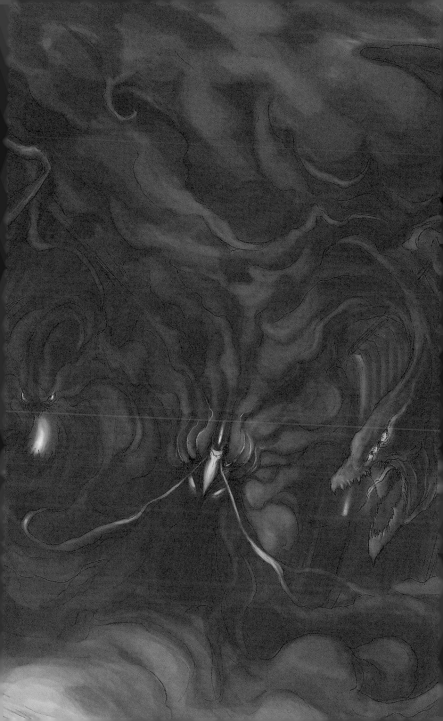

of them were driven by the sacred charge laid upon them by Ilúvatar, to care for his children. In this, the Valar resembled more closely the protective angels of some Christian folklore.

Tolkien describes how, after three ages of the Trees of Light, Morgoth feigned repentance and was released. However, he secretly created an alliance with Ungoliant the Great Spider, a female spirit whose closest analogue is perhaps the Hindu goddess Kali, 'she who is death'. Together they slew the Trees of Light, and Morgoth killed Finwë,

The Maiar Ossë and Uinen

King of the Noldor, and stole the Silmarilli jewels from the stronghold of Formenos.

As they held the only trace of the Light of the Trees left in Arda, these gems took on a symbolic significance that can be paralleled with relics of the True Cross in Christian folklore. Tolkien tells how Morgoth forged an iron crown and set it with the three radiant jewels; so it is interesting to note that one of the oldest and most famous crowns in Christendom is known as the Iron Crown of Lombardy. This heavily jewelled crown was worn

Ungoliant the Great Spider

by historic rulers from Charlemagne to Napoleon and takes its name from the claim that it has a central iron ringlet forged from a nail used in the crucifixion of Christ.

Morgoth achieved the corruption of the Noldor in two ways: firstly by going among them in fair form and revealing hidden knowledge, infecting them with pride and greed, and then by blatant murder and theft so cruel that Finwë's son Fëanor, maker of the Silmarils, was stirred to madness, and swore along with his seven sons a blasphemous oath of vengeance against any who would 'hold or take or keep a Silmaril'. Here Tolkien establishes one of his repeated themes: corruption and war through forbidden knowledge and unwarranted pride, a motif to which he would return with the influence of Sauron upon both the Númenóreans and the Elven-smiths in later ages.

As Tolkien observed in his letters, 'the first fruit of their fall is war in Paradise, the slaying of Elves by Elves'. Just as one son of Adam and Eve murdered his brother after their parents gained forbidden knowledge, so the Noldor slew the Teleri and stole their swan ships to pursue Morgoth to Middle-earth.

PART
TWO.

BATTLES OF THE FIRST AGE

THE
WAR
OF THE
JEWELS

———•———

THE FIRST BATTLE OF BELERIAND
DATE: AGES OF THE STARS

◄—————•———◄◄◄

THE BATTLE-UNDER-STARS
DATE: AGES OF THE STARS

◄—————•———◄◄◄

THE GLORIOUS BATTLE
DATE: 60 FIRST AGE

—◦—

LOCATION FOR ALL THREE: BELERIAND

———•———

The history of the War of the Jewels is the main focus of *The Silmarillion*, and as Tolkien wrote, 'the legendary *Silmarillion* is peculiar, and differs from all similar things that I know in not being anthrocentric. Its centre of view and interest is not Men but Elves.' Indeed, the War of the Jewels has its beginning before the origin of the human race. The arrival of the Noldor in Middle-earth surprised Morgoth; twice he sent his armies of Orcs to destroy them, and twice the Orcs were routed. In this, Tolkien showed us not

The Noldor returning to Middle-earth

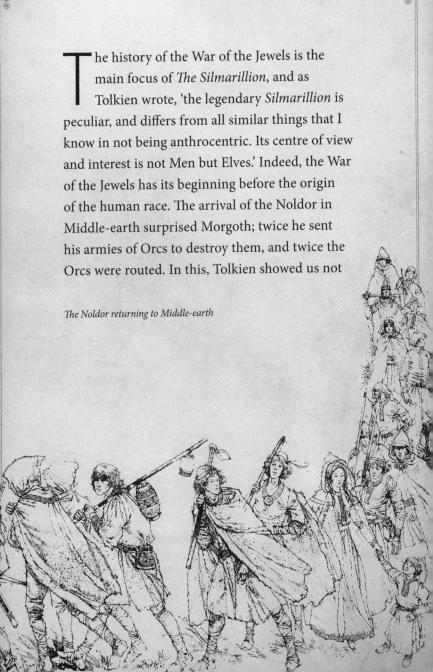

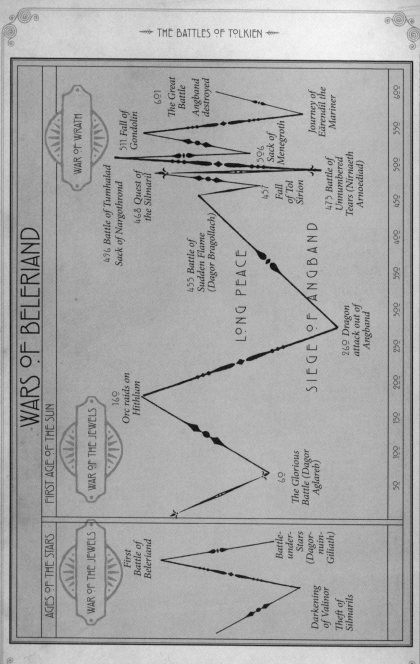

WARS OF BELERIAND

AGES OF THE STARS | FIRST AGE OF THE SUN

WAR OF THE JEWELS | WAR OF THE JEWELS | WAR OF WRATH

Darkening of Valinor
Theft of Silmarils

First Battle of Beleriand

Battle-under-Stars (Dagor-nuin-Giliath)

60 The Glorious Battle (Dagor Aglareb)

160 Orc raids on Hithlum

LONG PEACE

SIEGE OF ANGBAND

260 Dragon attack out of Angband

455 Battle of Sudden Flame (Dagor Bragollach)

457 Fall of Tol Sirion

473 Battle of Unnumbered Tears (Nirnaeth Arnoediad)

496 Battle of Tumhalad Sack of Nargothrond

468 Quest of the Silmaril

506 Sack of Menegroth

511 Fall of Gondolin

601 The Great Battle
Angband destroyed

Journey of Eärendil the Mariner

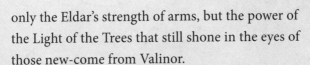

only the Eldar's strength of arms, but the power of the Light of the Trees that still shone in the eyes of those new-come from Valinor.

The tragedy of mortal Men is in their struggle against their ultimate fate of death. The tragedy of the immortal Elves is in their struggle with eternal life in a mortal world where nothing lasts, and all else changes and perishes.

In *The Silmarillion* we learn how the most gifted kindred of the Elves leaves the immortal paradise of Valinor and reenters the mortal lands of Middle-earth in a doomed attempt to reclaim the three Silmarilli jewels. And, as Tolkien observed in the history of the Elves of that age, 'the events are all threaded upon the fate and significance of the Silmarilli ("radiance of pure light") or Primeval Jewels'.

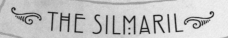

THE SILMARIL

THE SAMPO
AND THE GRAIL

The influence of Finnish language and literature on *The Silmarillion* has been considerable, and frequently stated by Tolkien. He wrote that the Finnish national epic, the *Kalevala*, was the germ of *The Silmarillion*.

The prizes of both epics seem equally obscure. In the *Kalevala*, the object that brings tragedy is called the Sampo. It is the work of the smith Ilmarinen, handed over as payment for a bride. When stolen back, it is broken in pursuit, and survives in fragments. Yet no one knows what it is – or rather, what it was, for its loss is irrevocable and complete. This is similar to the Silmarils, which were also forged by a master-smith, Fëanor the Noldo. Meanwhile, philologists suggest the Sampo is variously something bright, something made in a forge, a kind of mill, a thing that brings luck, or something to do with sea salt.

Some have suggested it is something like the

Golden Fleece, or even the Holy Grail, believed to
be the chalice used by Christ at the Last Supper. The
Grail, in many stories surrounding it, has become
an elusive and enigmatic symbol; it doesn't belong
to this world, as it is far too pure for mortal beings.
Only Galahad was pure enough to lift it, but then
both he and the Grail ascended straight to heaven.
Good in itself, the Grail ruined Camelot, and many
good knights died pursuing it. Tolkien surmised the
Sampo was at once both an object and an allegory –
real and abstract. He saw it also as the quintessence
of the creative powers, capable of provoking both
good and evil. His Silmarils were intended as objects
of similarly intense but obscure symbolism, focal
points of the inexorable pattern of fate.

   The Grail, the Sampo and the Silmarils all
serve as a reminder to the created beings that
the mystery of ultimate destiny and purpose was
something they could not penetrate. And yet they
all generated an ardent yearning to find them and
hold them, which led to much shedding of blood.
The paradox is that the gems shine with divine
light, yet for all who have pursued them, they have
provoked a descent into darkness and tragedy.

THE BATTLE OF SUDDEN FLAME

THE FOURTH BATTLE IN THE WAR OF THE JEWELS
DATE: 455 FIRST AGE

LOCATION: BELERIAND

I n the winter of the year 455 of the First Age, the Dagor Bragollach – the Battle of Sudden Flame – ended the Long Peace and broke the Siege of Angband. The battle was well named, for it was heralded by volcanic rivers of fire pouring out of Angband. The fire incinerated the Noldor troops in the hillforts and encampments on Ard-galen 'the green plain', which thereafter became known as Anfauglith, or 'the land of gasping dust'.

In the train of these rivers of fire came wave after black wave of Orcs led by Balrog fire demons and Morgoth's most terrible creation, Glaurung the Golden. Tolkien reveals the full force of Morgoth's evil genius with the appearance of the Father of Dragons and his dreadful brood. Tolkien's dragons are creatures of powerful and ancient evil, inspired by the brutal and primitive world of the earliest Old German epics.

In his 'On Fairy-Stories', Tolkien speaks of the inspiration for Glaurung: 'best of all was the nameless North of Sigurd of the Volsungs, and the prince of all dragons'. This 'prince of all dragons' was the spectacularly patricidal, fratricidal, genocidal and, in general, deeply unpleasant Fafnir the Fire-Drake, the usurper of the cursed golden treasure of the (mysterious and extinct) Nibelungs.

Yet, however evil the dragon is, Tolkien believed that 'the world that contained even the imagination of Fafnir was richer and more beautiful, at whatever cost of peril'. And so, at great peril to all the Free Peoples of Middle-earth, Glaurung appears in the Battle of Sudden Flame.

MAP OF THE BATTLE

The map on pages 54–55 is an artist's impression of the initial wave of destruction and chaos as the Siege of Angband is broken. For Tolkien's account of the conflict, see *The Silmarillion*, 'Of the Ruin of Beleriand and the Fall of Fingolfin'.

Glaurung

Glaurung at the Battle of Sudden Flame

FINGOLFIN MORGOTH WOLVES-WEREWOLVES ATTACK

ELVES ORCS-TROLLS GLAURUNG DEFENCE

EDAIN BALROG DRAGONS

PASS OF SIRION

DORTHONION

GONDOLIN

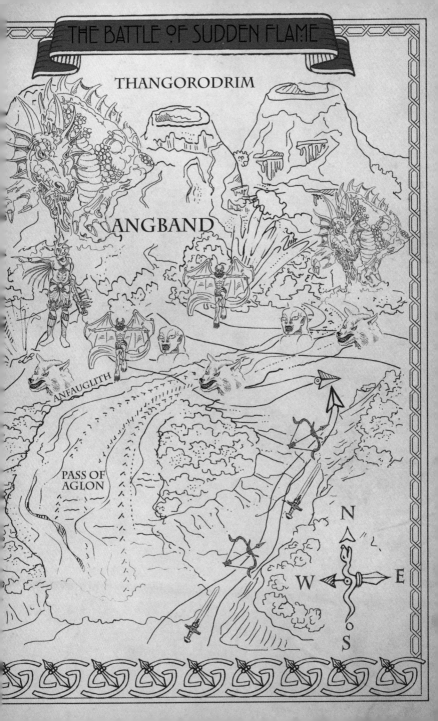

THE BATTLE OF SUDDEN FLAME

THANGORODRIM

ANGBAND

ANFAUGLITH

PASS OF
AGLON

N
W E
S

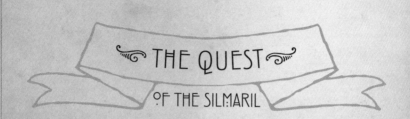

THE QUEST
OF THE SILMARIL

Tolkien seems to have blended classical and Celtic sources in the tale of Beren and Lúthien, which takes place in the dark years between the Battle of Sudden Flame and the Battle of Unnumbered Tears. One of the very first stories of Middle-earth to be written, and inspired by Tolkien's own great love – on his and his wife Edith's gravestone is written 'John Ronald Reuel Tolkien (1892–1973) Beren' 'Edith Bratt Tolkien (1889–1971) Lúthien' – this tale tells of how two lovers descend into the underworld.

Tolkien himself acknowledged that the story was based on the myth of Orpheus and Eurydice, with the male and female roles reversed. Orpheus played his harp and sang to make Cerberus the hound guardian fall asleep before the gates of Hades so that he could steal in and retrieve his beloved Eurydice, while the song of Lúthien lulled the wolf Carcaroth, so that she and Beren might descend into the pits of Angband

Morgoth, the Dark Enemy

and seek for a Silmaril. The song of Lúthien before Morgoth was a single combat as potent in its way as any duel of arms. Perhaps the most injurious to the fallen Vala's pride, as the lovers bested him in his very throne room, and 'together wrought the greatest deed that has been dared by Elves or Men'.

NEXT PAGE
Lúthien sings before Morgoth

THE BATTLE OF UNNUMBERED TEARS

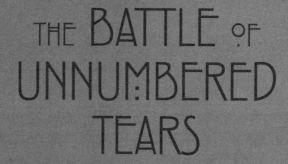

THE FIFTH BATTLE IN THE WARS OF THE JEWELS
DATE: 472 FIRST AGE

LOCATION: BELERIAND

The armies of Morgoth

In the Battle of Unnumbered Tears an alliance of Elves, Men and Dwarves made one last desperate attempt to overthrow Morgoth and reclaim Beleriand. With their utter ruin, Tolkien brought the atmosphere of Norse and Old German saga to bear in creating one of the grimmest times in the history of Arda.

It was in the long aftermath of the Battle of Unnumbered Tears that the bleakest and, yet,

Fingolfin, High King of the Noldor

grandest individual tragedy of the War of the
Jewels took place. In the tragic figure of the mortal
Túrin Turambar, nemesis of Glaurung, we have
the first of Middle-earth's dragon-slayers, whose
tale is rooted in Northern European epic. His
story is inspired both by the cursed hero Kullervo
from the Finnish *Kalevala* who unwittingly sleeps
with his long-lost sister and afterwards falls on his
sword, and Sigurd, who slays Fafnir the Prince of
Dragons by thrusting his sword into the creature's
soft underbelly. The tale of Túrin takes us into the
world of Northern European epic, with its bitter,
doomed heroes.

MAP OF THE BATTLE

The map on pages 64–65 is an artist's impression
of the Battle of Unnumbered Tears. For Tolkien's
account of the conflict, see *The Silmarillion*,
'Of the Fifth Battle: Nírnaeth Arnoediad'.

THE BATTLE OF UNNUMBERED TEARS

IRON MOUNTAINS

PASS OF SIRION

FINGON'S
WEST ARMY

MEN OF
BRETHIL AND
DOR-LÓMIN

DWARVES OF
BELEGOST

ORCS

TRO

MAEDHROS'
EAST ARMY

EDAIN

MORGOTH

WOLVES-
WEREWOLVES

EASTERLI

TURGON'S
GONDOLIN
ARMY

GWINDOR'S
NARGOTHROND
ARMY

BALROG

GLAURU

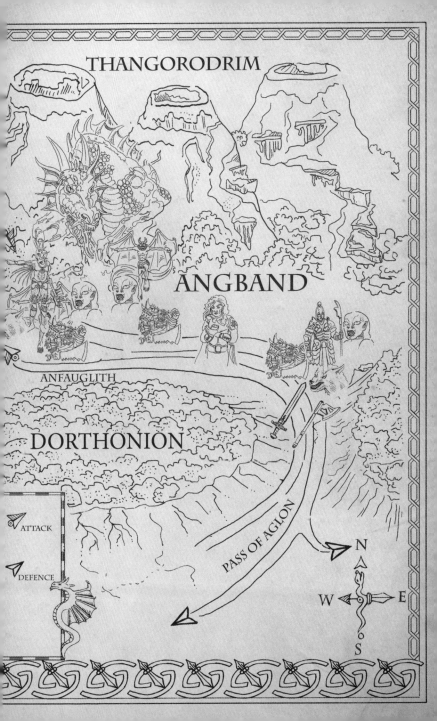

THANGORODRIM

ANGBAND

ANFAUGLITH

DORTHONION

PASS OF AGLON

ATTACK

DEFENCE

N
W E
S

As Tolkien wrote in a letter to W.H. Auden, '... the beginning of the legendarium [...] was in an attempt to reorganize some of the *Kalevala*, especially the tale of Kullervo the hapless, into a form of my own'.

One of the most desperate battles in the War of the Jewels took place in the ancient Sindarin kingdom of Doriath, as the Sons of Fëanor sacked the stronghold of Menegroth. So the oath that began the War of the Jewels led once more to Elf turning against Elf, and the corruptive lure of the gems culminated in ruin as the surviving sons pursued the Silmaril, borne now by Lúthien's granddaughter.

Yet, ultimately, Tolkien's use of these 'Primeval Jewels' is symbolically ambivalent, as it is the desire for the possession of the gems that results in disaster, while the Silmarils themselves remain symbols of ultimate good, the last remnant of the Trees. After long travels, the Silmaril of Doriath came to travel the skies in the winged ship Vingilot, becoming a beacon to Middle-earth and explaining, in Tolkien's cosmology, the origin of the morning and evening 'star' that we know as the planet Venus.

OPPOSITE PAGE
Túrin Turambar slays Glaurung the Father of Dragons

THE WAR OF WRATH

DATE: 587 FIRST AGE

LOCATION: BELERIAND

In keeping with their mingled roots in Greco-Roman mythology and the Christian concept of angels, the Valar had remained in the paradise of Aman yet never truly ceased to care for the sufferings of the Children of Ilúvatar. They acknowledged that the time had come to end the suffering and break the evil dominion of Morgoth over Middle-earth.

The War of Wrath, also known as the Great Battle, led to the breaking of the Iron Mountains

An army of Orcs

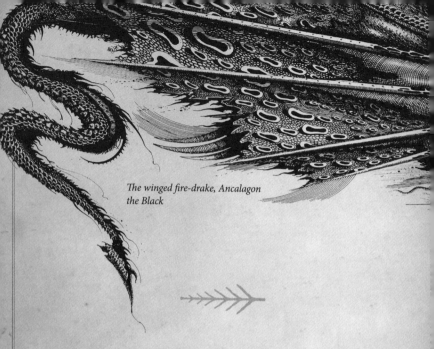

The winged fire-drake, Ancalagon the Black

and the sinking of Beleriand, bringing the 'Quenta Silmarillion' to its fated end in a conflict, which, Tolkien wrote, 'owes, I suppose, more to the Norse vision of Ragnarök than to anything else'.

And just as the final battle of Ragnarök began with the sounding of the Horn of Heimdall, the Watchman of the Gods, Tolkien's Great Battle of the War of Wrath begins with the blast of the Horn of Eönwë, the Herald of the Valar. Gothmog, Lord of Balrogs, bears a flaming sword into the Great Battle, as does the fire giant Surt in the Norse legend.

MAP OF THE BATTLE

The map on pages 72–73 is an artist's impression of the War of Wrath. For Tolkien's account of the battle, see *The Silmarillion*, 'Of the Voyage of Eärendil and the War of Wrath'.

IRON
MOUNTAINS

MANWË EDAIN VINGILOT GOTHMOG ANCALAG

EÖNWË DWARVES EAGLES BALROG ORCS-TROLLS

TULKAS ELVES MORGOTH SAURON WOLV

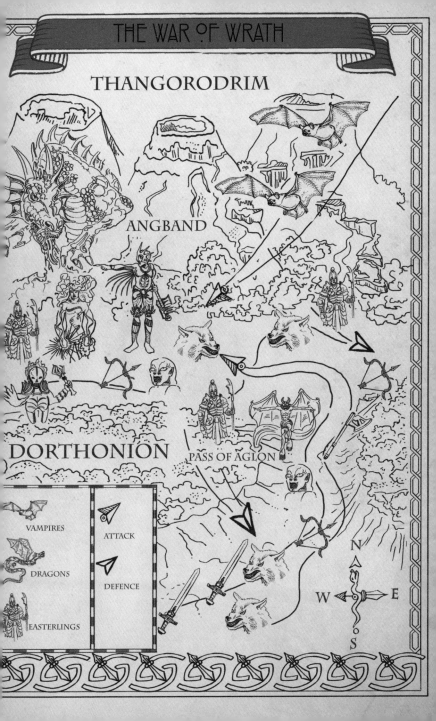

THE WAR OF WRATH

THANGORODRIM

ANGBAND

DORTHONION

PASS OF AGLON

VAMPIRES

ATTACK

DRAGONS

DEFENCE

EASTERLINGS

N

W E

S

PART

THREE

THE SECOND AGE

WARS
OF THE
ELVES
AND
NÚMENORÉANS

THE WAR OF SAURON AND THE ELVES

DATE: 1693–1701 SECOND AGE

LOCATION: ERIADOR

J
ust as Tolkien once observed that the history of the Elves of the First Age was linked to the fate and significance of the three Silmarilli jewels, so we see this theme recur in the history of the Elves and Men of the Second and Third Ages, which were linked to the fate and significance of the Rings of Power – also forged by the Elves.

Elven-smiths of Eregion

Further parallels can be drawn between the two stories as Tolkien's chosen chief protagonist among the Elves of this age was Celebrimbor, the grandson of Fëanor, who forged the Silmarils.

In Prometheus, the good Titan of Greek mythology who brought fire and light to the human race, we have a mirror opposite to Tolkien's Sauron, the evil sorcerer who brought death and darkness. However, in the Second Age, when Melkor's former lieutenant appeared in disguise as the mysterious Annatar the Lord of Gifts among the Elven-smiths of Eregion, he must have seemed to the Elves everything that Prometheus was to

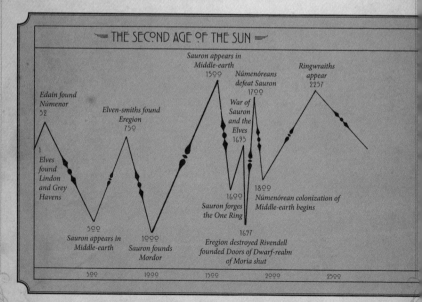

⟿ THE SECOND AGE OF THE SUN ⟿

Sauron appears in
Middle-earth
1500

Númenóreans
defeat Sauron
1700

Ringwraiths
appear
2251

Edain found
Númenor
32

Elven-smiths found
Eregion
750

War of
Sauron
and the
Elves
1693

Elves
found
Lindon
and Grey
Havens
1

500
Sauron appears in
Middle-earth

1000
Sauron founds
Mordor

1600
Sauron forges
the One Ring

1697
Eregion destroyed Rivendell
founded Doors of Dwarf-realm
of Moria shut

1800
Númenórean colonization of
Middle-earth begins

500   1000   1500   2000   2500

humans. For Annatar was a magician-smith who
– like Prometheus – defied the gods and gave
to them the great gift of forbidden knowledge
and skills, but for quite different purposes. With
Annatar's guidance, Celebrimbor and the Elven-
smiths of Ost-in-Edhil in Eregion learned skills of
forge and fire only matched by the Vala Aulë the
Smith. Only after the forging of the Rings of Power
did the Elves learn the terrible price of Annatar's
gifts. While in Greek mythology Prometheus's gifts
were freely given, Annatar's gift of the Rings of
Power would ultimately result in enslavement to
the terrible Lord of the Rings.

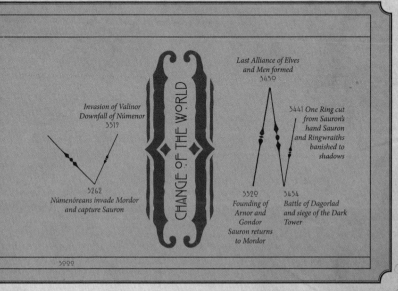

CHANGE OF THE WORLD

Last Alliance of Elves
and Men formed
3430

Invasion of Valinor
Downfall of Númenor
3319

3441 One Ring cut
from Sauron's
hand Sauron
and Ringwraiths
banished to
shadows

3262
Númenóreans invade Mordor
and capture Sauron

3320
Founding of
Arnor and
Gondor
Sauron returns
to Mordor

3434
Battle of Dagorlad
and siege of the Dark
Tower

3000

The walls of Khazad-dûm,
where they bordered on Eregion

WARS
OF THE
NÚMENÓREANS

DATE: SECOND AGE

LOCATION: NÚMENOR, MORDOR
AND THE LANDS BETWEEN

The island of Númenor, Tolkien's version of Atlantis

T he Second Age of the Sun was the era that saw the rise of the mighty Sea Kings of Númenor, the 'Land of the Star'. In High Elvish, the name of their kingdom was Atalantë, and it was Tolkien's version of Atlantis. Its rise and fall is a paradigm of the growth and demise of empires.

The myth of Atlantis is one of the most enduring in human history, an island realm that Tolkien believed had actually existed and endured in humanity's 'racial memory'. In Tolkien's case, this was manifest in a 'terrible recurring dream' of a 'Great Wave, towering up, and coming in ineluctably over the trees and green fields'.

His own 'great Atlantis isle of Númenorë' was a newly risen, star-shaped island in the Western Sea that lay between Middle-earth and the Undying Lands. The Númenóreans were greatly strengthened in body and mind by the Valar, yet although they were granted a lifespan many times that of other Men, and gifted with wisdom and skills, they were not without fault. In a letter written in the late 1950s, Tolkien wrote that the Númenóreans 'were proud, peculiar, and archaic, and I think are best pictured in (say) Egyptian terms.' So, too, we might observe that the ultimate fate of the Númenóreans had much in common with that of Pharaoh's army in its arrogant pursuit of the Hebrews of Moses.

It was Sauron who proved their downfall. In Tolkien's recurring motif of the deceiver who comes bearing gifts, this time the evil Maia allowed himself to be captured in the year 3262 of the Second Age rather than risk the Númenóreans destroying Barad-dûr.

Throughout Tolkien's chronicles, mortal Men are ruled by their consciousness of death, whether it is Denethor, Steward of Gondor, running defiantly to suicide, or the Númenóreans' obsession with prolonging life. Far more effective than any military strategy was Sauron's ability to sow dissent among men and convince them that their true enemies were the Elves and the Valar, who refused to share their secret of eternal life.

NEXT PAGE
Númenor disappears in the cataclysm

THE
LAST
ALLIANCE OF
ELVES AND MEN

DATE: 3434–3441 SECOND AGE

LOCATION: MORDOR

W hen the Last Alliance of Elves and Men marched on Mordor in 3434 of the Second Age, Tolkien framed the conflict in Arthurian terms.

In 2013 Tolkien's unfinished poem *The Fall of Arthur* was published, illuminating similarities between his conception of the Arthurian legends and the battles of the Second and Third Ages of Middle-earth. Many stanzas are strongly redolent of the threat of Sauron: 'The endless East in anger woke / and black thunder born in dungeons / under mountains of menace moved above them.' For the Battle of Dagorlad and the Siege of the Dark Tower, Tolkien seems to have drawn particularly on the legend of the Last Battle of Camlann. At Camlann, Arthur destroyed the forces arrayed against him, only for he and Mordred to slay each other in climactic single combat; the Alliance experienced a similarly pyrrhic victory as their armies triumphed but Gil-galad and Elendil received mortal wounds as they finally overcame Sauron.

After Arthur's death, it was the duty of one surviving knight to retrieve the king's sword.

In Tolkien's Middle-earth, it was left to Elendil's son Isildur to retrieve (the shards of) the king's sword and with it cut the One Ring from Sauron's hand.

MAP OF THE BATTLE

The map on pages 92–93 is an artist's impression of the Battle of Dagorlad and the Siege of the Dark Tower. For Tolkien's account of the battle, see *The Silmarillion*, 'Of the Rings of Power and the Third Age'.

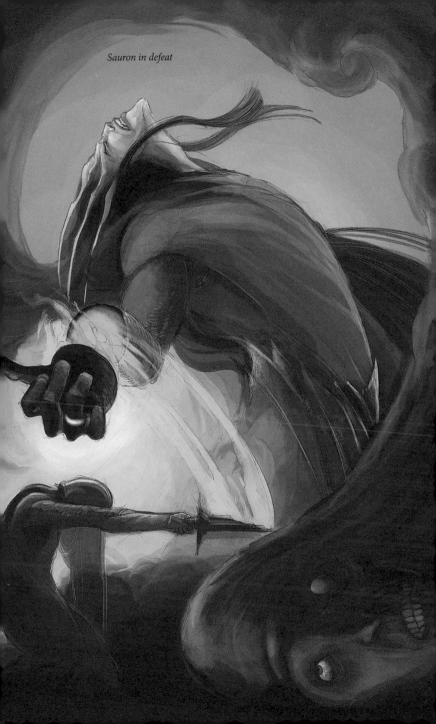

Sauron in defeat

DAGORLAD

BLACK
GATE

DEAD
MARSHES

TOWERS OF
THE TEETH

MOUNTAINS
OF SHADOW

THE BATTLE OF DAGORLAD AND
THE SIEGE OF THE DARK TOWER

MORDOR

GIL-GALAD	LAST ALLIANCE	SAURON	NAZGÛL			ATTACK
ISILDUR	ANÁRION	SILVAN ELVES	TROLLS			DEFENCE
ELENDIL	ORCS	SOUTHRONS	EASTERLINGS			

ASH MOUNTAINS

THE DARK
TOWER
(BARAD-DÛR)

MORDOR

PLATEAU OF
GORGOROTH

MOUNT
DOOM
(ORODRUIN)

N

W   E

S

PART
FOUR

WARS
OF THE
DÚNEDAIN

THE
DISASTER
AT
GLADDEN
FIELDS

DATE: 2 THIRD AGE

LOCATION: THE GLADDEN FIELDS,
BETWEEN MIRKWOOD
AND THE MISTY MOUNTAINS

OPPOSITE PAGE
The death of Isildur

⇝ THE NORSE LORD ⇜
OF THE RINGS

Tolkien was familiar with the concept of magical rings from Norse literature. Odin, the one-eyed sorcerer god whom Tolkien called 'the Goth, the Necromancer, Glutter of Crows, God of the Hanged', has much in common with Sauron – also called the Necromancer in *The Hobbit*. Odin possessed Draupnir, a great gold ring forged by the Elf-smiths of Alfheim. Its name meant 'the dripper' because it dripped eight gold rings of equal size and weight every nine days.

Draupnir provided the wealth and power by which Odin ruled the Nine Worlds of the Aesir and Vanir gods, dwarfs, men, dark elves, light elves, fire giants and frost giants. By possessing this Elf-forged gold ring, Odin was able to rule as the king of the gods.

Just as Sauron lost his ring in the war with the Last Alliance of Elves and Men, so Odin lost his at the funeral of his favourite son, Balder. As his

THE DISASTER AT GLADDEN FIELDS

VALES OF
ANDUIN

GREAT
RIVER
ANDUIN

GLADDEN
FIELDS

N

W — E

S

| | ISILDUR | | ISILDUR'S SONS | | ISILDUR'S BODY | | ATTACK |
| | DÚNEDAIN | | ORCS | | ISILDUR PUTS ON THE RING | | DEFENCE |

son's funeral ship was set alight and consumed in flames, Odin placed Draupnir on Balder's breast. Like Sauron, Odin's power was diminished without the ring. Like the One Ring, however, Draupnir was not destroyed, but went with Balder into the dark realm of Hel, the prison of the dead. And like Sauron sending out his Black Riders to recover the ring, so Odin mounted his eight-legged steed Sleipnïr, in order to reclaim Draupnir.

There is a third striking comparison between Odin and Sauron, and that is the motif of the single, solitary eye. In the Third Age, Sauron takes the form of a fiery, evil eye. In the Norse canon, we have Yggdrasil, the great ash tree also known as the World Tree, whose mighty limbs support the Nine Worlds. At Yggdrasil's foot is the Fountain of Wisdom, and it was there, thirsty for knowledge, that Odin went to drink. For one deep draught from the Fountain, Odin had to sacrifice an eye, which he did without hesitation. From that time on, he was always the One-eyed God.

Men of the Last Alliance: Elendil, Anárion and Isildur

MAP OF THE BATTLE

The map on page 99 is an artist's impression of the Disaster at Gladden Fields. For Tolkien's account of the skirmish and the death of Isildur the last High King, and the loss of the One Ring, see *The Silmarillion*, 'Of the Rings of Power and the Third Age' and *Unfinished Tales*, Part III, Chapter I.

⟫ THE THANGAIL ⟪

The 'thangail' shield wall for a double rank of heavy armed knights was one of Tolkien's own inventions that he attributed to the Númenóreans. Here Tolkien was drawing on real-world military history, as shield walls were an effective infantry strategy in warfare for thousands of years; however, their weakness was in the wall being outflanked, resulting in its collapse. Tolkien's thangail was a flexible shield wall capable even of curling around on itself and forming an unbroken circle of shields and spears, thus countering any attempt by the enemy to outflank the defenders.

Mount Doom, where the One Ring was forged

WARS OF THE NORTH KINGDOM OF ARNOR

DATE: 1300–1974 THIRD AGE

LOCATION: ARNOR

The greatest threat to the northern Dúnedain kingdom of Arnor was the war with Angmar and its Witch-king.

Tolkien did not invent the concept behind the Witch-king, that of a sorceror ruling by the supernatural power of a ring. From Mesopotamia through Scandinavia to China, the belief in the power of rings has been with the human race since the dawn of time. This is so much so that – in Northern Europe in particular – the quest for the ring is a pervasive theme in mythology. Even Tolkien's central concept of a 'War of the Ring' has a remarkable historical precedent.

The idea that an empire could be ruinously consumed by war because of a ring may appear an unlikely historical event. However, Tolkien had no less an authority than the ancient scholar Pliny to inform him that, in ancient Rome, a dispute over a ring caused a blood feud, which led directly to the outbreak of the Social Wars and the collapse of the Roman Republic.

The rise and fall of the Dúnedain kingdoms of Middle-earth likely owes much to Tolkien's intimate knowledge of the history of the Roman Empire. Certainly, Tolkien encouraged this comparison. To begin with, he created a landmass for the Dúnedain kingdoms that was roughly equivalent to that of France, Germany, Italy, Spain, Greece and the British Isles and Ireland combined.

Also, in an interview with a journalist in the 1950s, Tolkien spoke of the geography of his novels: 'the action of the story takes place in northwest of Middle-earth, equivalent in latitude to the coastlines of Europe and the north shore of the Mediterranean… If Hobbiton and Rivendell are taken (as intended) to be about the latitude of Oxford, then Minas Tirith, 600 miles to the south, is at about the latitude of Florence. The mouths of Anduin and the ancient city of Pelargir are at about the latitude of ancient Troy.'

The Barrow-wights sent by the Witch-king to dwell in the burial mounds of deserted Arnor

The Witch-king of Arnor, the greatest of the Nazgûl

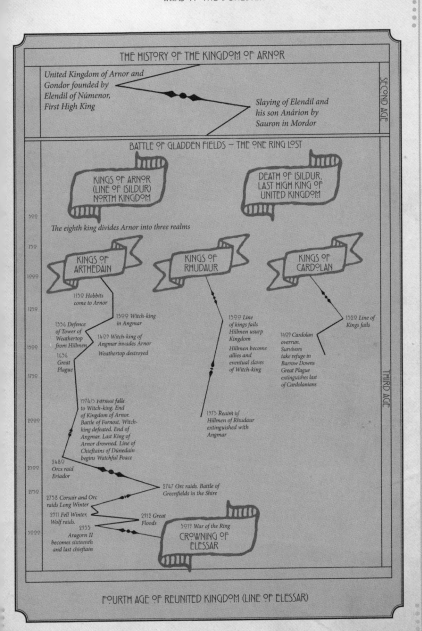

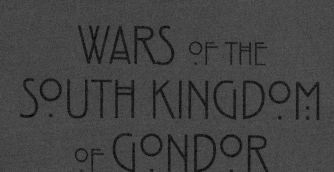

WARS OF THE
SOUTH KINGDOM
OF GONDOR

DATE: THIRD AGE

LOCATION: GONDOR

The history of Tolkien's South Kingdom of Gondor has even more in common with the chronicles of the Western Roman Empire than does that of the North Kingdom of Arnor. Just as the Roman Empire had to endure centuries of warfare with invading barbarians on its eastern borders, so the South Kingdom of the Dúnedain had to endure centuries of warfare from similar barbarian invasions from the east. Like those Asiatic invaders of the Roman world, the Easterlings of Middle-earth were a confederation of many kingdoms and races.

Gondorian guards

Many of the wars of Gondor are comparable to the early history of Rome in its long rivalry with Carthage over sea and land. Like Umbar, Carthage in North Africa commanded mighty fleets of warships, and allied itself with mercenary armies supported by war elephants and cavalries. And, although it was defeated after a century of war, Carthage's rivalry with Rome was later reawakened when it became the harbour for a powerful pirate fleet of sea raiders. Again, this is comparable to the history of the Corsairs of Umbar who for centuries raided the coasts of Middle-earth.

One of the most devastating incursions into Gondor was by a confederacy of Easterlings known as the Wainriders of Rhûn who, in 1851 of the Third Age, arrived in wagons and war chariots. This victory echoes the Visigoths' defeat of the Romans at Adrianople (AD 378). These wild tribesmen made their westward drive using horse-drawn wagons. They were not simply an army of raiders, but were described as 'an entire nation on the move in great wains' who came and occupied lands on the eastern borders of the Roman Empire.

Easterling tribesmen

In the resettlement of lands and the aftermath
of these battles as well, the histories of Rome and
Gondor reveal much in common. In gratitude for
the salvation of the Kingdom of Gondor in the
Battle of the Field of Celebrant, the Eóthéod, who
would later become the Rohirrim, were awarded
titles to the depopulated lands of Calenardhon.

Ships of the Corsairs of Umbar

Similarly, after the retreat of the invading Huns, the Goths became the main inheritors of the lands devastated by the barbarians of the Western Roman Empire. In both the Western and Eastern Roman Empires, the Goths – like the fictional Rohirrim – were given lands of their own as reward for their military services to a greater power.

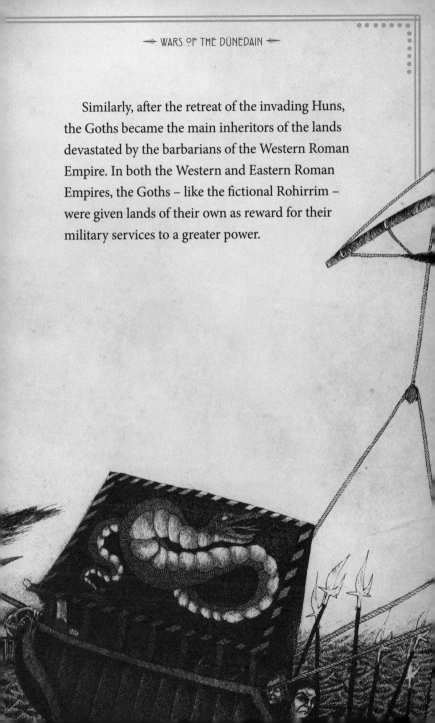

The Wainriders

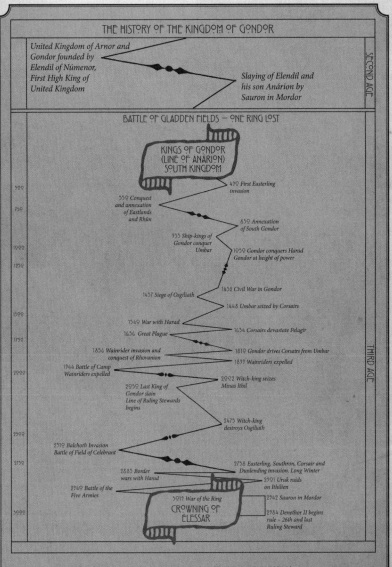

THE HISTORY OF THE KINGDOM OF GONDOR

United Kingdom of Arnor and Gondor founded by Elendil of Númenor, First High King of United Kingdom

Slaying of Elendil and his son Anárion by Sauron in Mordor

SECOND AGE

BATTLE OF GLADDEN FIELDS — ONE RING LOST

KINGS OF GONDOR
(LINE OF ANÁRION)
SOUTH KINGDOM

THIRD AGE

500

472 First Easterling invasion

750

550 Conquest and annexation of Eastlands and Rhûn

830 Annexation of South Gondor

933 Ship-kings of Gondor conquer Umbar

1000

1050 Gondor conquers Harad Gondor at height of power

1050

1437 Siege of Osgiliath

1432 Civil War in Gondor

1300

1448 Umbar seized by Corsairs

1540 War with Harad

1750

1636 Great Plague

1634 Corsairs devastate Pelargir

1856 Wainrider invasion and conquest of Rhovanion

1810 Gondor drives Corsairs from Umbar

1899 Wainriders expelled

2000

1944 Battle of Camp Wainriders expelled

2002 Witch-king seizes Minas Ithil

2050 Last King of Gondor slain Line of Ruling Stewards begins

2475 Witch-king destroys Osgiliath

2500

2510 Balchoth Invasion Battle of Field of Celebrant

2750

2758 Easterling, Southron, Corsair and Dunlending invasion. Long Winter

2885 Border wars with Harad

2991 Uruk raids on Ithilien

2942 Sauron in Mordor

2940 Battle of the Five Armies

3019 War of the Ring
CROWNING OF ELESSAR

2984 Denethor II begins rule – 26th and last Ruling Steward

3000

FOURTH AGE OF REUNITED KINGDOM (LINE OF ELESSAR)

PART

FIVE

THE THIRD AGE

WARS
OF THE
DWARVES

THE WAR OF
DWARVES
AND DRAGONS

DATE: THIRD AGE

LOCATION: THE NORTH OF MIDDLE-EARTH

The sagas of Northern Europe show a widespread belief in dwarfs as a powerful but stunted subterranean race that lived within mountains. They were also guardians of treasures and magical gifts, considered masters of fire and forge, and the makers of weapons and jewels.

Tolkien was dissatisfied with the portrayal of dwarfs in the fairy tales familiar to us today, and created his own race of Dwarves,* who

* Tolkien explained that he selected the plural 'Dwarves' for his imaginary people 'to remove them, a little, from the sillier tales of these latter days'.

A cold-drake of the north

were closer to those deep mythological roots. He felt that his Dwarves were comparable to the Norsemen of Scandinavia, that proud race of warriors, craftsmen and traders. Stoic and stubborn, both races were also relentless in their will to avenge perceived injustice. They were alike in their admiration of strength and bravery, in their sense of honour and loyalty, and in their love of gold and treasure. They were all but identical in their skill in the wielding and forging of weapons, in their stubborn pride, and their determination to avenge perceived injustice.

Dwarves are brave and fearless on their own ground, but distrustful and dismissive of all that they do not know. Unlike the Norsemen, they are fearful of the open sea.

Tolkien's writing was informed and inspired by his intimate knowledge of German and Norse myths that linked gold rings and gold hoards with dwarfs – and ultimately with dragons. In the *Nibelungenlied* and the *Volsunga Saga*, there are allusions to the myth of the gold ring known as Andvarinaut, the Ring of Andvari the Dwarf. It was also called 'Andvari's Loom' because of its

PREVIOUS PAGE
Dwarf arms and armour

Scatha the Worm

power to reproduce itself eternally. It was believed to be the source of the cursed Nibelung and Volsung treasures guarded by Fafnir the Fire-Drake, to whom Tolkien gave the epithet 'prince of all dragons'.

Yet, in Middle-earth, we also find that Tolkien remains consistent with ancient folk tradition:

The Battle of Azanulbizar

his Dwarves are the genii of the mountains, just as
Hobbits are the genii of tilled soil and farmlands,
and Ents are the genii of the forests. Through
his research, Tolkien felt that he was able to
understand fully the true nature and character of
this secretive, stunted, mountain-dwelling race.

In Tolkien's world, there is also continuous
conflict between Dwarves and Orcs – their
fellow underground dwellers. Dwarves make
dangerously persistent enemies, as proved by the
War of the Dwarves and the Orcs (2795–2799 TA)
that ended with the bloody slaughter of the
Battle of Azanulbizar. It is a conflict with echoes
in various mining cultures, from Cornwall to
China, where goblins or demons have been said to
sabotage miners in tunnels, hindering their work
out of sheer malice and spite.

THE BATTLE OF
THE FIVE ARMIES

DATE: 25 NOVEMBER 2941 THIRD AGE

LOCATION: EREBOR, THE LONELY MOUNTAIN

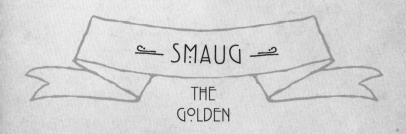

SMAUG

THE GOLDEN

I n 'On Fairy-Stories', Tolkien's celebrated lecture on the art and tradition of fairy tales, he wrote that 'The dragon had the trade-mark "Of Fairie" written plain upon him'. Tolkien believed that dragons and their golden hoards were to be found buried deep in the heartland of 'Fairie'. Certainly, these spectacular monsters enriched the imagination of the creator of Middle-earth, as he once declared: 'I desired dragons with a profound desire.'

When writing his fairy-tale adventure *The Hobbit*, Tolkien decided that a dragon was not only desirable but essential to his novel. Not just any dragon would do. In the creation of Smaug the Golden, we see a villain of great charm, intelligence and vanity as well as brute strength. Smaug is the last and greatest winged fire-drake of the Third Age: a fire-breathing flying dragon whose wrath and vengeance is somehow both terrible and magnificent.

The destruction of Esgaroth by Smaug the Golden

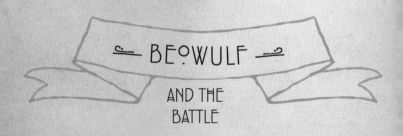

BEOWULF

AND THE
BATTLE

As a professor of Anglo-Saxon literature and an expert on the Old English epic poem *Beowulf*, J.R.R. Tolkien did not have to look far to discover inspiration for his monster. On first inspection, there are no obvious similarities between *The Hobbit* and *Beowulf*. There are strong parallels, however, in the plot structure of the dragon-slaying episode in *Beowulf* and the dragon-slaying episode that is found in *The Hobbit*. Beowulf's dragon awakes when a thief enters the monster's den.

The thief steals a jewelled cup from the treasure hoard as he flees for his life. Tolkien adapts this scene into Bilbo Baggins's burglary of Smaug the Golden's treasury where he steals a jewelled cup from the treasure hoard. Both thieves avoid being cuptured, escaping the anger of the dragons themselves. In both tales, it is the nearby settlements that suffer the dragon's wrath.

It is up to their respective champions, Beowulf in the Old English epic, and Bard the Bowman in *The Hobbit*, to slay the beast. Both heroes succeed in slaying their dragons, but at a cost. It seems that, to some considerable degree, *The Hobbit* relays the *Beowulf* dragon scene, but told from the thief's point of view.

Of course, there are differences: Bard survives to become King of Dale, while the older Beowulf does not long survive the conflict. Although victorious, Beowulf dies of his wounds. However, Beowulf's death is mirrored in *The Hobbit* not by Bard, but by that other warrior king of the tale, Thorin Oakenshield, who is also victorious in the Battle of the Five Armies, but dies of wounds sustained on the field.

BEORN

THE SKIN-CHANGER

The huge Northman Beorn, Chieftain of the Beornings (the 'man-bear' people) is a 'skin-changer': Tolkien's fairy-tale version of the bear-cult hero of the real-life berserker warrior cult ('bear-sark' or 'bear-shirt') of the Germanic and Norse peoples. Although the historical berserkers felt possessed by the ferocious spirit of the enraged bear, these states were only rituals attempting to imitate the core miracle of the cult: the incarnate transformation of man to bear. Yet Tolkien provides the real thing when Beorn has a battlefield transformation from fierce warrior into an enraged were-bear (though Tolkien never uses that word) – an event that turns the tide of battle.

Orc head on a spike

BATTLE TACTICS

Tolkien's Dwarves resembled the warriors of Norse myth in their fighting style. For example, in Thorin Oakenshield's sudden entry into the Battle of the Five Armies, the Dwarf-king employed an ancient Norse shock tactic in a formation known as the Svinfylking, or 'swine array'. This was a wedge-shaped shield-wall formation frequently used by heavily armed Viking warriors to break through enemy lines and create panic among the closed ranks of an army with superior numbers. It could be extremely effective, but it entirely depended on the initial monumental shock. If this flying wedge did not immediately break through enemy lines, the formation would soon collapse. Like many shield-wall tactics, it could often be outflanked and entirely encircled. And, indeed, this would likely have been the fate of Thorin Oakenshield and his warriors had it not been for the sudden arrival of an unexpected ally.

THE EAGLES

The Eagles of Middle-earth are generally not prominent players in Tolkien's narratives, but their intervention is nearly always crucial – as in the Battle of the Five Armies – and they arrive at times of desperate need, frequently when rescue can be achieved only by the power of flight. One has a sense that – even though they may not be physically present through much of the action, the spirit of these Great Eagles senses all and enables them to turn up exactly at the most critical moments: as vehicles of destiny, an interloping deus ex machina. They are part of a tradition of eagle-emissaries in myth, leading from the birds of the Greek god Zeus (the Roman Jupiter) to the vassals of Manwë, the Lord of the Winds of Arda.

MAP OF THE BATTLE

The map on pages 138–139 shows an artist's impression of the Battle of the Five Armies. For Tolkien's account of the conflict, see *The Hobbit*, Chapters XI and XVII, and *Unfinished Tales*, Part Three, Chapter III.

Thorin Oakenshield

THE LONELY MOUNTAIN

GATE OF EREBO

RUINS OF DALE

THORIN'S COMPANY	GANDALF	BILBO BAGGINS	BATS	ATTACK
ELVES	EAGLES	DWARVES OF IRON MOUNTAINS		DEFENCE
MEN	BEORN	WOLVES AND WOLF-RIDERS	ORCS	

THE BATTLE OF THE FIVE ARMIES

The Battle of the Five Armies

PART

SIX

THE
WAR
OF THE
RING

⟶ THE WAR ⟶
OF THE RING

Tolkien's *The Lord of the Rings* is an epic fantasy that in large parts presents the world as a battleground between the forces of good and evil. But these forces are not simplistic ones, and at the story's core is a moral struggle that results from a creative wish to acquire power to transform the world – and how that desire may lead to corruption of the soul.

It is also concerned with the nature of evil. In *Morgoth's Ring*, J.R.R. Tolkien and Christopher Tolkien attempt to differentiate between the two dark lords, thus defining two categories of evil: destruction and domination. The evil of Morgoth was bent upon outright destruction: 'Just as Sauron concentrated his power in the One Ring, Morgoth dispersed his power into the

Minas Morgul

very matter of Arda, thus the whole of Middle-earth was Morgoth's Ring.' However, the evil of Sauron as the Lord of the Rings was far weaker in its overall power, but far more focused and efficient. This evil of the Necromancer crushes the will and overwhelms the mind of an enemy. Its purpose is not destruction but domination – that is, enslavement of the mind and submission of the spirit to the tyranny of the Dark Lord of Mordor.

The Witch-king of Morgul

BATTLES OF THE WAR OF THE RING

3019	THIRD AGE
25 FEBRUARY	First Battle of the Fords of Isen
2 MARCH	Second Battle of the Fords of Isen
	March of Ents on Isengard
3/4 MARCH	Battle of the Hornburg
11 MARCH	Invasion of East Rohan
	First assault on Lórien
13 MARCH	Battle of Ships at Pelargir
	Battle under the Trees in Mirkwood
	Second assault on Lórien
15 MARCH	Battle of Pelennor Fields
17 MARCH	Battle of Dale
	Siege of Erebor
22 MARCH	Third assault on Lórien
25 MARCH	Battle before the Black Gate of Mordor
	One Ring destroyed in fires of Mount Doom
	Downfall of Sauron and Mordor
27 MARCH	Siege of Erebor broken
28 MARCH	Destruction of Dol Guldur in Mirkwood
1 MAY	Crowning of King Elessar
3 NOVEMBER	Battle of Bywater in the Shire
	Final downfall of Saruman
	END OF THE WAR OF THE RING

THE
BATTLE
ON THE
BRIDGE
OF
KHAZAD-DÛM

DATE: 15 JANUARY 3019 THIRD AGE

LOCATION: THE MINES OF MORIA (KHAZAD-DÛM)

The Battle on the Bridge of Khazad-dûm between Gandalf the Grey and the Balrog of Moria appears to have been inspired by a famous episode in Ragnarök: the final battle between the gods and the giants, which Tolkien specifically cited as the main influence on the earlier War of Wrath.

In *The Lord of the Rings*, the Balrog with his whip and sword of fire duels with Gandalf with his sword of cold white flame on the narrow stone bridge over the chasm of Moria. This is a diminished form of the titanic struggle between the fire giant Surt and Freyr, the god of sun and rain, on Bifröst, the Rainbow Bridge of Asgard. Both battles begin with the blast of a great horn: the Norse Horn of the Aesir, blown by Heimdall; and the Horn of Gondor, blown by Boromir. Both battles seem to end in disaster – both bridges collapse, and both sets of combatants hurtle down in a rage of flame to their doom.

The encounter between Gandalf and the Balrog is a breaking point in more than one way. Literally, of course, the stone bridge collapses as the wizard is dragged down into the abyss. The quest itself is taken beyond the point from which there can be any return. They can only go onward now.

⌐ MORAL ALCHEMY ⌐

Gandalf understands that, ultimately, the only way to defeat Sauron and his evil One Ring is not to attempt to overthrow him or to seize its power, but to undo the alchemical process by which the Ring of Power was made – just as common folklore tells us one can undo a spell by reciting it backwards.

We see in this the 'backward' nature of the ring quest. Only where it was forged can the One Ring be unmade, and Sauron's power destroyed.

Gandalf stands his ground against the Balrog

❧ BALROGS ❧

The most terrible of the corrupted spirits who became the servants of Melkor were the Maiar fire demons, or 'Balrogs'. Although Balrogs were known the carry the mace, axe or flaming sword, their chief and most feared weapon was the many-thonged whip of fire. Tolkien's Balrogs were wild and destructive fire demons, not unlike the Furies, the enraged spirits of vengeance who had snakes for hair, carried flaming torches, and used whips to beat their victims.

In many mythologies, there are evil volcanic spirits who live like the Balrogs deep in the roots of mountains. Medieval Christians often saw volcanoes as the vents of the fires of Hell. For the ancient Greeks and Romans, volcanoes were perceived as fires of the smith god Hephaestus (or Vulcan), where the wild spirits of earth and fire were tamed or enslaved by the Olympian gods and turned to more useful purposes at the forge.

Tolkien appears to have been greatly impressed

by the fire spirits found in Norse and Anglo-Saxon mythology. Their Midgard was a 'Land of Men' which was similar to Tolkien's Middle-earth. Northern Midgard was closed in by a land of frost giants, while the south was a land of fire giants. This demonic land of fire was called Muspellsheim. It was Muspellsheim that provoked Tolkien's imagination in his creation of his extraordinary demons of fire, the Balrogs.

MAP OF THE BATTLE

The map on pages 154–155 is an artist's impression of the Battle on the Bridge of Khazad-dûm. For Tolkien's account of the battle, see *The Lord of the Rings*, Book II, Chapter V.

THE BATTLE ON THE BRIDGE OF KHAZAD-DÛM

MISTY MOUNTAINS

SECOND HALL

THE FELLOWSHIP
OF THE RING

GANDALF

BALROG

ORCS

TROLLS

ATTACK

DEFENCE

ZIRAK-ZIGIL

4. BATTLE OF PEAK

3. BATTLE OF ENDLESS STAIR

MINES OF MORIA

1. BATTLE OF BRIDGE

2. FALL INTO ABYSS

ABYSS

N
W E
S

The confrontation on the bridge

THE
BATTLE
OF THE
HORNBURG

DATE: 3-4 MARCH 3019 THIRD AGE

LOCATION: HELM'S DEEP, IN THE WHITE MOUNTAINS

King Théoden of Rohan

MAP OF THE BATTLE

The map on pages 160–161 is an artist's impression of the Battle of the Hornburg. For Tolkien's account of the battle, see *The Lord of the Rings*, Book III, Chapter VII.

SARUMAN'S ARMY

ÉOMER'S MEN

ATTACK

HUORNS

THÉODEN'S HOUSEHOLD

DEFENCE

GANDALF AND ERKENBRAND

WHITE MOUNTAINS

THE HORNBURG

HELM'S GATE

DEEPING STREAM

HELM'S DEEP

THE BATTLE OF THE HORNBURG

DEEPING COOMB

HUORN WOOD

HELM'S DIKE

THE GORE

N
W E
S

Saruman's armies attack Helm's Deep

Riders of Rohan

THE WHITE WIZARD

AND THE BLACK

In Norse myths and Icelandic sagas, we can see one of the primary sources of inspiration for Tolkien's fictional world of Middle-earth. However, there is a fundamental difference between the Norse Midgard and Tolkien's Middle-earth. The Norse mythic world is essentially amoral, while Tolkien's world is consumed by the great struggle between the forces of good and evil. Consequently, the attributes of the Norse world's greatest wizard, Odin, are necessarily split in two in Tolkien's morality tale: the 'good' aspects of Odin are found in the wizard Gandalf, and the 'bad' aspects are found in the wizard Sauron.

The entire epic tale of *The Lord of the Rings* is primarily about the struggle for control of the world by these conflicting powers as embodied in this duel between the white wizard and the black wizard. And Tolkien's single great message – entirely foreign to the philosophy and aspirations of the Norsemen – is that 'power corrupts'.

The Lord of the Rings is about the corruption implicit in a quest for pure power, and how the pursuit of power is itself evil. We learn that, even when that power (as embodied in the ultimate power of the One Ring) is pursued for reasons that appear essentially 'good', it will necessarily corrupt the quester.

We see Gandalf's wisdom and strength of will in his refusal to take possession of the One Ring for a single moment, for fear of his own corruption. He knows full well that he would be morally destroyed by it as surely as others who have tried to harness its power, no matter how good and sound their intentions.

In the Quest of the Ring, we witness the corruption of Saruman, who originally was a 'good' wizard but who demonstrated the classic moral error of believing 'the end justifies the means'. In attempting to overthrow the forces of the evil Sauron, Saruman gathers forces that are just as evil, and is himself corrupted by the desire for power. Unwittingly, Saruman becomes the mirror image and ally of the evil being he initially wished to overcome.

However, by no means was everything in Tolkien's universe fixed as morally and simply 'black' or 'white'. Such rigidity would have prevented much exploration of character and development of the story. The most significant case in point is that of Saruman, who at the beginning of *The Lord of the Rings* is represented as one of the forces for good – indeed, as head of the White Council. At first, Gandalf himself has no doubts of Saruman's virtue and good intentions. Eventually, it becomes all too clear that Saruman, for all his gifts, becomes corrupted. Power, the great seducer, has affected even him. Tolkien was very conscious of power and of the responsibility and self-discipline that ought to go with it. His most admirable leaders, such as Aragorn and Faramir, wear their power lightly or keep it cloaked.

Saruman fails the test; his freedom to choose has led him in the wrong direction. But then, of course, the pursuit of power is the mainspring of the whole saga: and it is the One Ring that sets all the events in *The Lord of the Rings* in motion.

THE MARCH OF THE ENTS ON ISENGARD

DATE: 2-4 MARCH 3019 THIRD AGE

LOCATION: ISENGARD

Treebeard

Tolkien was an unashamed worshipper of trees. From childhood, he had admired and loved these ancient life-forms and believed that they were in some way sentient beings. When once asked about the origin of his Ents, Tolkien wrote: 'I should say that Ents are composed of philology, literature and life. They owe their name to the "eald enta geweorc" of Anglo-Saxon.' The Anglo-Saxon reference, meaning 'old giants' work', is to a fragment of a hauntingly beautiful Old English poem, 'The Wanderer'. The phrase related to the prehistoric stone ruins considered to be the work of an ancient lost race of giants.

However, beyond *ent* being an Anglo-Saxon name for 'giant', the inspiration for Tolkien's March of the Ents came about in a rather negative way: through his dislike and, indeed, disapproval of William Shakespeare's treatment of myths and legends. His greatest abuse was heaped on one of the playwright's most popular plays, *Macbeth*.

The creation of the Ents, Tolkien explained, 'is due, I think, to my bitter disappointment and disgust from schooldays with the shabby use made in Shakespeare of the coming of "Great Birnam wood to high Dunsinane hill": I longed to devise a setting in which the trees might really march to war.' Tolkien felt Shakespeare had trivialized and misinterpreted an authentic myth, providing a cheap, simplistic interpretation of the prophecy of this march of the wood upon the hill.

So in *The Lord of the Rings* Tolkien did indeed devise such a setting. And certainly, in his own March of the Ents, the fundamental opposition between spirits of the forest and of the mountain was revealed and portrayed in a way that lends power and dignity to the archetypal miracle of a wood marching on a hill.

To find beings of myth who do correspond directly to the Ents, Tolkien had only to look back into English folklore, where the Green Man plays a distinctive part. Green Man stories and carvings were common in Tolkien's beloved West Midlands and the Welsh Marches just beyond. He was a Celtic nature spirit and tree god who represented the coming of new growth in victory over the powers of ice and frost. Essentially benevolent, he could also be powerful and destructive.

The semi-sentient Huorns, who inspire such terror in Saruman's Orcs, represent the wilder, more dangerous aspect of the Green Man: an inhuman power tapping the deepest sources of the natural world where fowls, animals and even children were sacrificed to placate the demonic spirit of certain trees.

The appearance of Huorns brought terror to their foes. They may have been Ents who in time had grown treeish, or perhaps trees that had grown Entish, but they were certainly wrathful, dangerous and merciless. In the Huorns, we have a dramatization of an avenging army of 'Green Men' making an attack on all creatures who are hostile to the spirits of forests. Tolkien's trees really do march towards the citadel of their enemy, Saruman, whose servants have been despoiling the forest to feed the furnaces of Isengard.

MAP OF THE BATTLE

The map on pages 176–177 is an artist's impression of the March of the Ents on Isengard. For Tolkien's account of the fall of Isengard, see *The Lord of the Rings*, Book III, Chapters IX and X.

The tower of Orthanc

THE MARCH OF THE ENTS ON ISENGARD

'WIZARD'S VALE
(NAN' CÚRUNIR)

TREEBEARD
ORCS
WOLVES
ENTS
URUKS
DUNLENDINGS
SARUMAN
SARUMAN'S ARMY
ATTACK
DEFENCE

ORTHANC

MISTY MOUNTAINS

RIVER ISEN
(DAMMED)

RING OF
ISENGARD

ISENGARD

N
W E
S

The Ents attack Isengard

THE
BATTLE
OF THE
PELENNOR
FIELDS

DATE: 15 MARCH 3019 THIRD AGE

LOCATION: PELENNOR FIELDS

The city of Minas Tirith

The Battle of the Pelennor Fields is the most richly described conflict in the annals of Middle-earth, and the most dramatic, if not the final, battle of the War of the Ring. As such, it draws on many aspects of real-world military history, ranging over a thousand years of European warfare.

In his chronicles of Gondor and Arnor, Tolkien links the history of the Dúnedain kingdoms to many comparable aspects in the history of the ancient Roman Empire. However, by the time of the War of the Ring, in Aragorn's attempt at restoration of the Reunited Dúnedain Kingdom of Arnor and Gondor, Tolkien has drawn on the historical precedent of the warrior king Charlemagne, who reunited and restored the Roman Empire to its former glory in the form of the Holy Roman Empire in the 8th century.

In a letter to a publisher, Tolkien makes direct reference to this Carolingian motif in *The Lord of the Rings*: 'The progress of the tale ends in what is far more like the reestablishment of an effective Holy Roman Empire with its seat in Rome.'

And certainly, in its physical geography, Tolkien saw the Reunited Kingdom as an expanse of land comparable to Charlemagne's empire. The

Warriors of Gondor

action of *The Lord of the Rings* takes place in the
northwest of Middle-earth, in a region roughly
equivalent to the Western European landmass.
Hobbiton and Rivendell, as Tolkien often
acknowledged, were roughly intended to be at the
latitude of Oxford.

Gandalf strikes at the Witch-king at the gate of Minas Tirith

By his own estimation, this put Gondor and Minas Tirith some 600 miles (1,000 km) to the south in a location that might be equivalent to Florence. This would suggest that Mordor might be approximately comparable to the mountainous regions of Romania or Bulgaria and the basin of the Black Sea.

In terms of enemies as well as allies, Charlemagne and Aragorn have much in common. At the Battle of the Pelennor Fields, the Gondor and Rohan cavalry encounters an enemy in the form of the Southron cavalry of Harad. This is comparable to battles in which Charlemagne's cavalry fought their historic enemies: the Moors of Spain and the Saracens of North Africa. Other foes of Gondor and Rohan were the ancient, rebellious Dunlending tribesmen who had their

MAP OF THE SIEGE OF MINAS TIRITH

The map on pages 186–187 is an artist's impression of the Siege of Minas Tirith. For Tolkien's account of the siege, see *The Lord of the Rings*, Book V, Chapter IV.

THE SIEGE OF MINAS TIRITH

MINAS TIRITH

GANDALF ORCS NAZGÛL ROHIRRIM ATTACK

GROND URUKS EASTERLINGS DEFENCE

SOUTHRONS TROLLS WITCH-KING

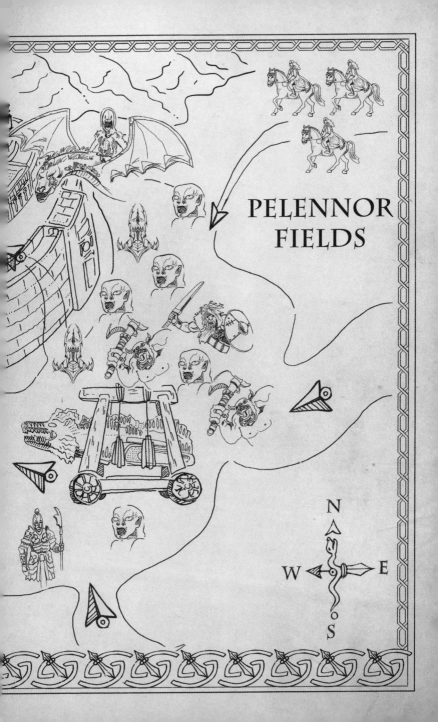

PELENNOR
FIELDS

N
W E
S

historical counterparts in the rebellious Basque tribesmen who ambushed Charlemagne's chevalier Roland in Roncesvalles Pass in the Pyrenees.

However, with the appearance on the Pelennor Fields of the warriors mounted on Mûmakil – equivalent to Hannibal's Carthagian war elephants – and companies of Easterlings bearded like Dwarves and armed with great two-handed axes – equivalent to the late Byzantine axe-bearing infantries – Tolkien introduces troops and weaponry drawn from both much earlier (3rd century BC) and much later periods (12th century AD) of European warfare.

And, as already noted, Tolkien's dramatic charge of the Rohirrim in the Battle of the Pelennor Fields has parallels with the 5th-century Roman account of an historical Gothic cavalry action in the Battle of Châlons in AD 451. This was an alliance between the Roman general Flavius Aetius and the Gothic King Theodoric that proved to be the salvation of Western Europe from the seemingly unstoppable invading hordes of Attila the Hun.

Similarly, among earlier allies of Mordor, we are told, there were the Easterlings of Rhûn who were perhaps inspired by the 12th-century Seljuk Turks of Rhum (Anatolia). Meanwhile, among those fighting on Gondor's eastern borders were the Variags of Khand; these were perhaps inspired by the 10th- or 11th-century Variangians of the Khanate of Kiev, who were also known as the Rus – and, later, the Russians.

The charge of the Rohirrim

MAP OF THE BATTLE

The map on pages 196–197 is
an artist's impression of the
Battle of the Pelennor Fields.
For Tolkien's account of the
event, see *The Lord of the
Rings*, Book V, Chapters V
and VI.

Éowyn of Rohan

∽ THE SHIELDMAIDEN ∽

AND THE NAZGÛL

For Tolkien's inspiration for the death of the Witch-king we must once again look to the plays of William Shakespeare. First, there is Tolkien's choice of date for the Witch-king's imminent death on 15 March: the Ides of March, the first day of the old Roman calendar that was also the fatal date of Julius Caesar's assassination. The Witch-king, as he turns from Gandalf and the gate to join battle on Pelennor Fields, would have been well advised by Shakespeare's soothsayer to 'Beware the Ides of March.' And second, in Tolkien's portrayal of the Black Captain and Lord of the Ringwraiths, we have a mortal man who has sold his immortal soul to Sauron for a ring of power and the illusion of earthly dominion. This tragic exchange, set within the context of his epic fantasy world, was exactly comparable to Shakespeare's *Macbeth*: the tale of a king who has lost his doomed and blasted soul.

The life of the Witch-king is protected by a prophecy that is almost identical to the final one that safeguards Macbeth. Tolkien's Witch-king 'cannot be slain by the hand of man', while the similarly deluded Macbeth 'cannot be slain by man of woman born'.

The Witch-king is, of course, not slain by the hand of man but by the shieldmaiden Éowyn of Rohan. Here again, Tolkien draws on ancient historical and mythological traditions that feature warrior maidens.

Aragorn sails to Minas Tirith

*The Dead Men of Dunharrow
come to the aid of Aragorn*

WHITE MOUNTAINS

MINAS TIRITH

RIVER ANDUIN

PORT OF HARLOND

THÉODEN

ARAGORN

ÉOWYN

NAZGÛL

EASTERLINGS

URUKS

ATT

MÚMAKIL

WITCH-KING

ORCS

DEF

TROLLS

IMRAHIL'S
FORCES

ROHIRRIM

SOUTHRONS

THE BATTLE OF THE PELENNOR FIELDS

PELENNOR FIELDS

RAMMAS ECHOR

N
W   E
S

Éowyn slays the Witch-king

THE
BATTLE
OF THE
BLACK GATE

DATE: 25 MARCH 3019 THIRD AGE

LOCATION: THE PLAIN OF DAGORLAD, BEFORE MORDOR,
MIDDLE-EARTH

The Dark Tower
of Mordor

*A Mûmak – a war elephant of
the armies of Harad (who fought
with Sauron), bearing war towers
upon their backs*

Tolkien's *The Lord of the Rings* has much in common with legends in many cultures throughout the world, in which heroes or villains possess 'external souls' that are kept hidden within objects outside the body. The legends spring from a number of sources. However, when the soul is kept in a metal object such as a ring, one can be certain that the source of the legend is the tradition of the magician-smith.

The epic hero Gesar of Ling is a remarkable example of this tradition. Gesar was a warrior, magician, smith and king who ruled a great mountain kingdom. The epic events of Gesar's life demonstrate the ancient belief that not only can individual souls or lives be kept in a ring or metal talisman, but so can the souls or lives of entire dynasties and whole nations. This certainly parallels Tolkien's epic adventure, where Sauron the Dark Lord's entire evil empire collapses with the One Ring's destruction.

The multi-skilled hero Gesar becomes the King of Ling by virtue of many feats of heroism and magic. His confirmation as king comes when the supernatural guardians of the kingdom allow

MAP OF THE BATTLE

The map on pages 206–207
is an artist's impression of
the Battle of the Black Gate.
For Tolkien's account of the
conflict, see *The Lord of the
Rings*, Book VI, Chapter X.

*One of the Olog-hai, a race of gigantic
intelligent trolls*

him entry into a crystal mountain where the treasures of Ling are kept. Without doubt, the most important is the emblematic throne of the realm, on which rests a huge gold mandala ring that is known as the 'Life of Ling' with a crystal vessel at its centre, from which flow the shining 'waters of immortality'.

Although born a royal prince, while he is still a child his parents are slain by Kurkar, an evil sorcerer and the King of Hor. With his inherited powers of sorcery, the orphaned Gesar becomes an extraordinary smith. He forges an unbreakable sword from celestial (meteoric) iron.

Gesar prepares himself for his ultimate duel with his great enemy, the King of Hor. However, he knows that Kurkar cannot be slain until a huge iron mandala ring is destroyed. This huge iron ring contains the 'life' or 'soul' of Kurkar and all his ancestors: 'It is the "life" of my ancestors. Sometimes it speaks.' However, Kurkar believes he is safe because the iron ring cannot be melted or forged by any known means. The fire of the furnace does not even redden the sacred iron.

But Gesar is no ordinary smith, and he summons his supernatural brothers and a multitude

THE BATTLE OF THE BLACK GATE

SOUTHRONS

ARMY OF
THE WEST

SAURON

NAZGÛL

ATTA

GANDALF

ORCS AND
URUKS

TROLLS: OLOG-HAI

DEFE

EAGLES

MOUTH OF
SAURON

EASTERLINGS

The Nazgûl in flight

of spirits to work in a huge volcanic forge. Gesar and his supernatural brothers strike the iron mandala with hammer blows that sound like thunder. At last the iron 'life of the Kings of Hor' is broken, although we are told that 'the three worlds shook' with its destruction. Once this has been achieved, Gesar of Ling takes up his sword of celestial iron and, with a single stroke, cuts off the sorcerer's head.

In Tolkien's *The Lord of the Rings*, Sauron the Ring Lord shares many characteristics with both Gesar of Ling and Kurkar of Hor. Like Gesar of Ling, Sauron is both a supernaturally gifted smith capable of creating unmatched wonders in his forge, and a magician capable of terrifying acts of sorcery. Both have mountain strongholds and both must keep safe the golden rings by whose powers they rule their kingdoms.

At this point, the comparison between Gesar of Ling and Sauron of Mordor largely ceases. Sauron the Dark Lord is much more closely allied in values to the evil King of Hor. Kurkar, like both Gesar and Sauron, also has a ring or talisman that must be kept safe and by whose power he rules his kingdom. However, Kurkar's iron talisman is

much more like Sauron's One Ring because both are inherently evil, and the sorcerers' lives depend on the survival of the rings. Kurkar's iron ring of Hor also shares the One Ring's characteristic of being almost indestructible. Normal fires do not even cause the metal in them to redden. Both require supernatural fires of volcanic intensity to melt them down.

The destruction of Kurkar's iron ring of Hor in Gesar's volcanic forge-room causes a cataclysm in which 'the three worlds shook'. Not to be outdone, this is matched by the climax of *The Lord of the Rings*, when the destruction of Sauron's One Ring in Mount Doom's volcanic forge-room causes a comparable cataclysm in which 'the earth shook, the plain heaved and cracked, and… the skies burst into thunder seared with lightning'.

Gesar is a warrior-king who is both a smith and a magician. To such a hero, all things are possible. He assumes many forms, creates invulnerable weapons, conjures up phantom armies and creates wealth and prosperity for his people.

In Asian myth and history, the connection between alchemy or metallurgy and the power of

Legolas Greenleaf

NEXT PAGE
The Mountains of Mordor

kings and heroes is often more obviously stated than it is in Europe. Tradition insists, for instance, that the great historic Mongol conqueror, Genghis Khan, was descended from a family of smiths. So, too, was the legendary Tartar hero Kok Chan, who possessed a ring that – like Sauron's One Ring – hugely increased his already formidable powers.

The idea is suggested or implied in European ring quest epics like the *Volsunga Saga* and the *Nibelungenlied*, but the point is more often made explicit in Asian epic tales. Perhaps this is because Eastern religions or philosophies, such as Buddhism, are not in conflict with their shamanistic traditions. Nor do they appear to have a Christian tendency to vilify or eliminate these traditions.

This ancient magician-smith tradition was nonetheless powerfully influential in Northern Europe. Its strongest manifestation is found in the mythology of the Finno-Ugric people of Finland and Estonia. The supreme manifestation of their

PREVIOUS PAGE
The destruction of Mordor

culture is the national epic of Finland, known as
discovered in his youth and acknowledged had
had a profound influence on him in the shaping of
his own cosmology.

THE BATTLE OF
BYWATER

DATE: 3 NOVEMBER 3019 THIRD AGE

LOCATION: BYWATER, THE SHIRE

The Lord of the Rings began as the fairy-tale sequel to *The Hobbit* and evolved into high chivalric romance on an epic scale. However, the difference between the traditional tale of chivalric romance and that of *The Lord of the Rings* is its perspective and its choice of hero.

Traditionally, Frodo Baggins would simply have been a foil to Aragorn. The Hobbit would have been considered too frail – and all too human – to be a likely candidate for the role of the questing hero. Aragorn is large, strong and almost superhuman in his fearlessness and virtue.

In the end, however, it is the 'ordinary' human qualities of compassion and humility in the Hobbit that are finally what is required to prevail in this particular quest. The deep wisdom of compassion found in the human (or Hobbit) heart succeeds where heroic strength cannot.

A Hobbit bowman

In the chronicles of Middle-earth at the end of the Third Age, it soon becomes apparent that the acts of greatest courage were achieved by the smallest of protagonists. Time and again, almost unnoticed, Hobbits perform acts of bravery that prove critical to the turning of the tide of great events in Middle-earth. This can be seen, for instance, in Bilbo Baggins's role in the slaying of Smaug the Dragon, in Meriadoc Brandybuck's acts in the slaying of the Witch-king, and in Samwise Gamgee's mortal wounding of Shelob the Great Spider.

In the end, it is the humble Frodo Baggins, not the noble Aragorn, who achieves the Ring Quest. Frodo's moral courage is as remarkable as his endurance.

In the penultimate chapter of *The Lord of the Rings*, Tolkien draws a clear link between petty tyranny, exploitation and bullying, and the larger forms of evil of the world. After Saruman is defeated and ruined as the all-powerful wizard of the White Hand of Isengard, he is humbled and deprived of his supernatural powers, but retains his evil desire to dominate, hurt and destroy on a very petty level. And the author allows him to inflict this evil upon the place nearest to his own

Farmer Cotton and the Chief's Men

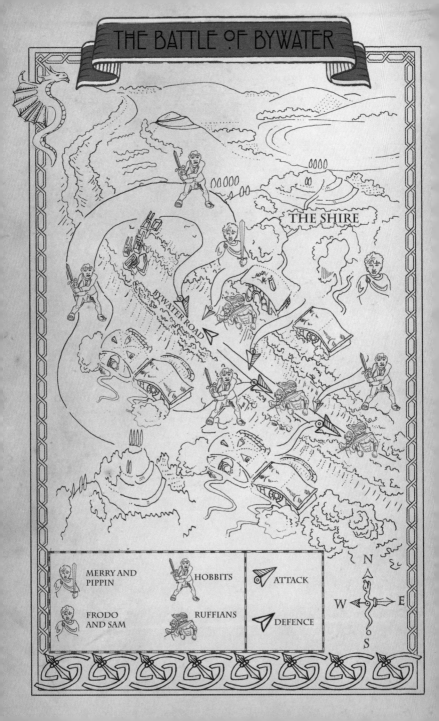

THE BATTLE OF BYWATER

THE SHIRE

BYWATER ROAD

MERRY AND
PIPPIN

HOBBITS

ATTACK

FRODO
AND SAM

RUFFIANS

DEFENCE

N
W — E
S

heart in the Hobbit lands of the Shire.

Tolkien once claimed to be a Hobbit in
everything but height. His Shire was modelled
on an idealized rural West Midlands of his
early childhood years that remained among his
most cherished memories. Tolkien wrote of the
importance of his heritage both in his imaginative
fiction and his academic work: 'I am indeed in
English terms a West Midlander at home only in
the counties upon the Welsh Marches; and it is, I
believe, as much due to descent as to opportunity
that Anglo-Saxon and Western Middle English
and alliterative verse have been a childhood
attraction and my main professional sphere.'

In the Shire we have something akin to an
Edwardian ideal of rural 'Merry Old England' that
in the wake of war has been ruined by greed and

MAP OF THE BATTLE

The map on the opposite page is an artist's
impression of the Battle of Bywater. For Tolkien's
account of the conflict, see *The Lord of the Rings*,
Book VI, Chapter VIII.

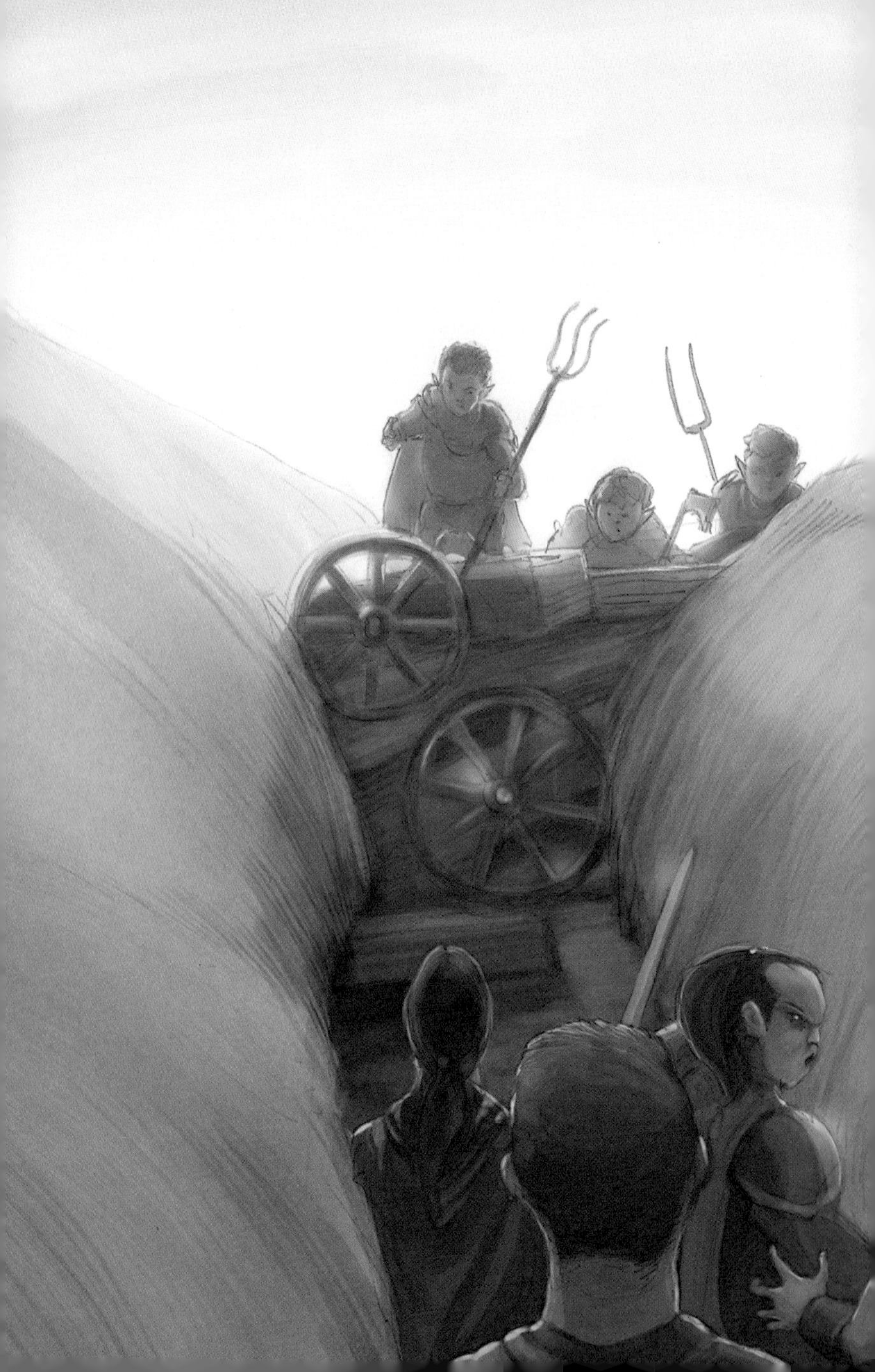

petty tyranny. The Shire's largely passive rural folk are betrayed by one of their own in collaboration with the enemy: the ruin of the Shire is as intrinsic to Tolkien's story as any other episode. 'The Scouring of the Shire' brings the message home to the reader that no place is safe from the disasters of war – and that the moral failures which allow evil to exist in everyday places like the Shire are the same that allow evil to prevail in the wider worlds. In both, it takes courage and conviction to resist and overthrow them.

Although the Battle of Bywater is recorded as the last battle in the War of the Ring, it was not by any means a great military event. It was essentially a series of skirmishes that resulted in fewer than a hundred deaths, but it brought the moral message of the war to the doorstep of the Hobbits of the Shire. 'This is worse than Mordor!' said Sam. 'Much worse in a way. It comes home to you, as they say: because it is home, and you remember it before it was all ruined.'

Meriadoc Brandybuck, Esquire of Rohan, and Peregrin Took, Knight of Gondor

The Death of Saruman

Peace once again in the Shire

WAR AND HONOUR

n J.R.R. Tolkien's spectacular accounts of battles and wars of Middle-earth, we see a deeply committed Christian who was nonetheless fascinated by extremely warlike pagan civilizations. In the warrior societies of his pagan ancestors, Tolkien saw much that was admirable: codes of honour, oaths of allegiance, astonishing acts of courage. Those codes later became formalized in the chivalric tradition endorsed by medieval knights and warrior kings. Tolkien understood chivalry as a later evolution of what he called the 'noble spirit of the north' tamed and civilized by Christianity. To Tolkien, Charlemagne was also the embodiment of the 'noble spirit of the north', but, unlike Aragorn, the emperor's nobility had been sanctified and brought to a greater purpose and glory. It was in what Tolkien called the 'theory of courage' that he expressed the most admiration for his ancestors. Tolkien wrote of 'the theory of courage, which is the greatest contribution of early Northern literature'.

Life was seen as hostile, while death was something dark, cold and without consolation. The world of the ancient Anglo-Saxon gave no quarter to gods, let alone men. Tolkien knew that the Northern gods were on the side of right and nobility, but in that world they are not the team that wins. The gods and heroes are defeated by the monsters and swallowed up in the eternal dark – only tales of their heroic deeds remain (and then only as long as the tribe or the poets' words survive). As Tolkien once observed, although the gods are defeated, the rough philosophers of these people believed that defeat was the fate of all mortals, and eventually even the fate of the gods themselves. It was simply a matter of finding a defiant and honourable means of departing when the moment came.

This was something that Tolkien, as a Christian, would not agree with, but there is something curiously familiar – and contemporary – about Tolkien's discussion of his 'theory of courage' as applied to men in a pre-Christian era of darkness and chaos. In fact, it resonated with that indifferent universe of contemporary literature that was concerned with life after the 'death of God' – 20th-century existentialist literature that Tolkien believed he had spent his entire life successfully avoiding.

Existential authors also looked to mythology for an analogue to the modern condition. Albert Camus found it in the myth of Sisyphus condemned to an external, meaningless, repetitive task without consolation or reward of any kind. As Tolkien himself acknowledged, the fate of all men is ultimately death. And honour does not lie in victory. Honour is gained in facing life with brutal honesty and finding 'a potent but terrible solution in naked will and courage'. These are Tolkien's words, but they could have been the words of Camus or any of the most radical existential writers of his day. It is a philosophy that is both ancient and – for Tolkien – disturbingly modern.

NEXT PAGE
Eärendil the Mariner

A CHRONOLOGY OF THE KINGDOMS ON

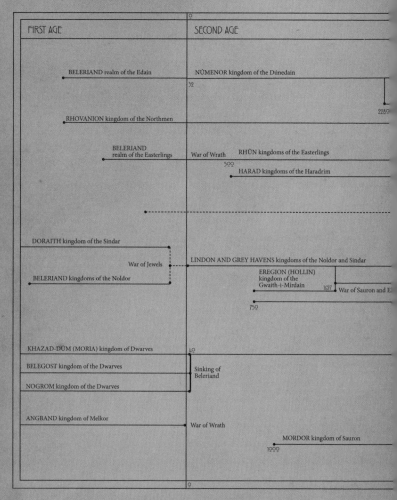

FIRST AGE	SECOND AGE
BELERIAND realm of the Edain	NÚMENOR kingdom of the Dúnedain
	32
	2280
RHOVANION kingdom of the Northmen	
BELERIAND realm of the Easterlings	War of Wrath RHÛN kingdoms of the Easterlings
	500
	HARAD kingdoms of the Haradrim
DORAITH kingdom of the Sindar	
War of Jewels	LINDON AND GREY HAVENS kingdoms of the Noldor and Sindar
BELERIAND kingdoms of the Noldor	EREGION (HOLLIN) kingdom of the Gwaith-i-Mírdain 1697 War of Sauron and E
	750
KHAZAD-DÛM (MORIA) kingdom of Dwarves	40
BELEGOST kingdom of the Dwarves	Sinking of Beleriand
NOGROM kingdom of the Dwarves	
ANGBAND kingdom of Melkor	War of Wrath
	MORDOR kingdom of Sauron
	1000

THE REALMS OF MEN, HOBBITS, ELVES

MIDDLE-EARTH IN THE AGES OF THE SUN

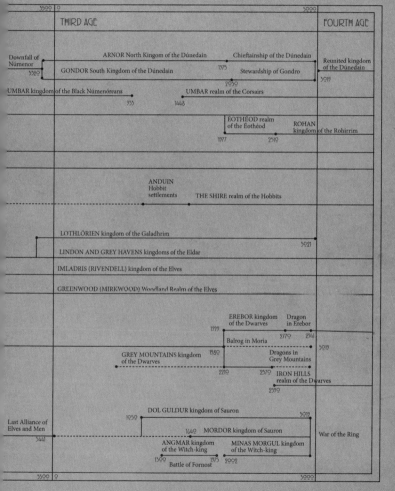

5500 0		5000
	THIRD AGE	FOURTH AGE

Downfall of Númenor 3320

ARNOR North Kingom of the Dúnedain

Chieftainship of the Dúnedain 1975

GONDOR South Kingdom of the Dúnedain

Stewardship of Gondro 2050

Reunited kingdom of the Dúnedain 3019

UMBAR kingdom of the Black Númenóreans 933

UMBAR realm of the Corsairs 1448

ÉOTHÉOD realm of the Éothéod 1977

ROHAN kingdom of the Rohirrim 2510

ANDUIN Hobbit settlements

THE SHIRE realm of the Hobbits

LOTHLÓRIEN kingdom of the Galadhrim 3021

LINDON AND GREY HAVENS kingdoms of the Eldar

IMLADRIS (RIVENDELL) kingdom of the Elves

GREENWOOD (MIRKWOOD) Woodland Realm of the Elves

EREBOR kingdom of the Dwarves 1999

Dragon in Erebor 2770 2941

Balrog in Moria

GREY MOUNTAINS kingdom of the Dwarves 1980

Dragons in Grey Mountains 2210 2570

IRON HILLS realm of the Dwarves 2590 3019

DOL GULDUR kingdom of Sauron 1050 3019

Last Alliance of Elves and Men 3441

MORDOR kingdom of Sauron 1640

War of the Ring

ANGMAR kingdom of the Witch-king 1300 Battle of Fornost 1975

MINAS MORGUL kingdom of the Witch-king 2002

| 5500 0 | | 5000 |

DWARVES AND THE DARK POWERS

INDEX

PAGE NUMBERS IN ITALIC TYPE REFER
TO ILLUSTRATIONS AND TABLES

Mirkwood

Mirkwood